Diary of a Wimpy Vamp nester Fiction City.

Adventures of a Wimpy Werewolf

HAIRY BUT NOT SCARY

Tim Collins is originally from Manchester, and now lives in London. He is the author of twelve books including *Diary of a Wimpy Vampire*, which won the 2011 Manchester Fiction City award, and *Diary of a Wimpy Vampire: Prince of Dorkness*.

Find out more about Tim at his website:
www.timcollins.com

Adventures of a Wimpy Werewolf

HAIRY BUT NOT SCARY

TIM COLLINS

Michael O'Mara Books Limited

First published in Great Britain in 2011 by
Michael O'Mara Books Limited
9 Lion Yard
Tremadoc Road
London SW4 7NQ

A CIP catalogue record for this book is available from the British Library.

Papers used by Michael O'Mara Books Limited are natural, recyclable products
made from wood grown in sustainable forests. The manufacturing processes
conform to the environmental regulations of the country of origin.

ISBN: 978-1-84317-856-9 in paperback print format
ISBN: 978-1-84317-858-3 in EPub format
ISBN: 978-1-84317-857-6 in Mobipocket format

1 2 3 4 5 6 7 8 9 10

www.mombooks.com

Designed and typeset by Envy Design
Illustrations by Andrew Pinder

Printed and bound by CPI Group (UK) Ltd, Croydon, CR0 4YY

ACKNOWLEDGEMENTS

Thanks to Collette Collins, Kate Moore, Andrew Pinder,
Lindsay Davies, Louise Dixon and Ana McLaughlin

Adventures of a Wimpy Werewolf

Monday 9TH April

It's five in the morning and I've just woken up to find my bedroom trashed. My bookshelf is overturned, my games are scattered all over the floor, and my revision notes are in shreds.

It must have been a burglar. What if they're still in the house?

I should go and fight them. I should dish out some vigilante justice.

On second thoughts, I think I'll just wait here a little bit first.

Adventures of a Wimpy Werewolf

This is weird. I've just been downstairs and found that nothing was damaged. No windows were broken, no locks were forced and nothing was missing.

I think I did the damage myself. What other explanation can there be?

I've worked it out now. I must be a sleepwalker. Oh God, why is this happening now, so soon before my exams? Okay, I need to calm down. I'm sure this was a one-off incident brought on by revision stress. School starts again today. I need to forget about it.

This morning I strolled into school as though nothing had happened. I'm not the sort of weirdo who trashes their room in the night, I told myself. I'm a fifteen-year-old with excellent grades predicted in my exams, who has earnt the respect of my peers.

As I walked through the school gates, Tyson from my class shouted: 'Gingernut!'

Okay, that bit about the respect of my peers isn't entirely true. But it should be. I'm a prefect and I'm president and founding member of both the chess club and the debating club. And yet my immature schoolmates insist on hurling abuse about the colour of my hair.

We have a tradition at our school where everyone puts their hands around their necks and shouts 'Choke!' if you don't reply to an insult quickly enough. To avoid this, I've prepared a number of comebacks:

Them: 'Oi! Carrot top!'
Me: 'Actually the top of a carrot is green, not orange.'

Them: 'You've been drinking too much Sunny Delight.'
Me: 'Sugary drinks don't affect hair colour, although they can cause acne and obesity, so perhaps you're the one who's been drinking them.'

Them: 'Is Ron Weasley your mum?'
Me: 'No. Is Hagrid yours?'

Soon none of this will matter. My ignorant schoolmates will fail their exams and head for the nearest dole office, while I'll go on to sixth-form college, university and a glorious career in politics. And my first act will be to make teasing someone about their hair colour an official hate crime.

Adventures of a Wimpy Werewolf

Tuesday 10TH April

I've just woken up from a really horrible nightmare.
I was opening a birthday present from Auntie Susan
and Uncle Derek. When I tore off the wrapping I saw it
was a packet of dog biscuits. I'm usually quite good at
pretending to like terrible presents. But in my dream,
the gift sent me into a snarling rage and I.. sort of...
ate them. It was really graphic. If it had been shown
on television I'd have written in to complain about the
unacceptable level of violence.

   Then I imagined I woke up and my body was so long
that my feet went right off the end of the bed and
my pyjamas were stretched to breaking point. But that
must have been part of the dream, of course.

Adventures of a Wimpy Werewolf

Maybe I'm still dreaming now. Maybe in a minute I'll somehow find myself in my old primary school with the man from the newsagent's and Gandalf.

I need to get a grip. I think I'll memorize the periodic table. That will make everything better.

We had a lesson about the Treaty of Versailles in History today and I'd read ahead in my textbook so I could answer all the questions.

After a brief introduction, Mr Jordan asked if anyone knew the terms of the treaty. I knew them all, and was just about to answer when I noticed my hands were covered in thick ginger hairs.

It was so weird. The hairs hadn't been there when I moisturized this morning. And yet now it looked like I was wearing mittens.

The worst thing is, I find really hairy people disgusting. I was once served an ice cream by a man with really

Adventures of a Wimpy Werewolf

hairy knuckles and I couldn't eat the cone because he'd touched it.

I shoved my hands into my armpits and listened in frustration as my ignorant classmates attempted to guess the terms of the treaty. I wished I could put my hand up, but I knew my pride at answering the question would be cancelled out by the shame of my hairy mitts.

A few minutes later, the patches of hair had gone. How can that have happened? Did I imagine it? Is exam stress making me hallucinate now?

My friend Pete once told me that the government puts chemicals in the water supply to control our minds. Maybe that's why I'm hallucinating. Maybe the government has found out about my political ambitions and they're suppressing me through tap water.

No, that's silly. I'm just getting paranoid. I think I'll stick to bottled water for the time being, though.

14

Wednesday 11TH April

I had another really horrible dream last night. In this one I was chasing the ginger cat from number 23 through a forest at night. I was running on all fours, with my face close to the ground, and following the feline scent. I caught up with the cat, and was just about to bite its throat when my alarm woke me up.

For a moment, it felt like my whole body was shrinking. Then Mum came in to ask what was wrong. She said I'd been howling so loudly it had woken her up, which is odd because she usually sleeps through anything.

I was leaving our front gate this morning when I saw the postman approaching. I smiled and greeted him as I always do, but then I had a really strong urge to keep him out. For some reason, part of my brain told me I needed to do everything I could to keep him off our territory, whether that meant scratching him or biting his throat. I ignored this bizarre urge and carried on down the street.

Why did I want to attack him? I'm not a violent person. So far my adolescence has been relatively calm, but now it seems I'm turning into one of those difficult teens you see on BBC3.

I think I know what's happening to me. I think I've been possessed by the devil. I knew I shouldn't have downloaded all that heavy metal from iTunes. I only did it because Pete said it was cool. This is what happens when you go along with peer pressure. I'm going to delete it all right now.

Thursday 12TH April

I slept right through the night, thankfully. No nightmares, no signs of damage and no hallucinations about shrinking. It looks like deleting those Iron Maiden albums did the trick. I might even download some Cliff Richard to make sure the devil doesn't possess me again.

It turns out my problems aren't over at all. In fact, they're getting worse.

I broke my blazer in Maths today. I still don't quite know how it happened, but I think my back grew to an enormous size and then shrank again.

I was trying to get my head around a trigonometry question, but I just couldn't do it. I started to worry about what I'd do if a question like that came up in my final exam in June.

What if I ended up getting just a plain A rather than

an A star? Even worse, what if I got a B? What if I failed maths? What if I failed all my exams and had to get a job as a cleaner? I'd have to spend the rest of my life tracing out right-angled triangles in the dirt and remembering the day it all went wrong.

For a split second, it felt as if my back was being pulled in all directions at once by some kind of torture device. I tipped out of my chair, slamming my head into the side of the desk. But then it was over, leaving me with just a torn shirt and blazer to deal with.

I crawled back into my seat as everyone in the class did the shame coughs. 'Shame coughs' are a tradition we have in our school where you pretend to cough but really shout the word 'shame'. That way you can say you were just coughing if the teacher tries to give you a detention for disrupting the class.

As far as the class was concerned, I'd done nothing more than fall out of my chair in a fit of maths-related overexcitement. But I know my back almost doubled in size. I wasn't imagining it. My ripped clothes prove it.

As I was leaving today, the headmaster, Mr Landis, stopped me and asked who ripped my blazer. I pretended

I'd caught it on a peg in the corridor, but he wasn't having it.

He demanded to know which member of Tyson's gang had done it. When I refused to name anyone, he gave me a lecture about how it was my role as a prefect to ensure that peer pressure didn't win out over school pride. I was one of just seven pupils who still wore the regulation school blazer, and I mustn't let the

Adventures of a Wimpy Werewolf

bullies stop me. I told him I'd do my best to mend the blazer and return to full school uniform as quickly as possible.

I was going to ask Mum to mend my blazer tonight, but I didn't want to explain what happened. I've only got a couple of months of school left anyway, so I think I'll throw what's left of it away.

It's a shame, though. I really liked that blazer. I deliberately chose one that was Teflon-coated so if anyone spat or drew a crude picture on it, I could wipe it clean and the joke would be on them.

I think I understand what's happening to me now, although it's very difficult to face up to.

One night last month, I popped down to the corner shop to buy some milk for Mum. On the way home, I was attacked by a large dog. I can't remember much about it now, but at the time I felt as though I was being so savagely mauled that I was going to die. I crawled back down the street, intending to call an ambulance as soon as I got home.

Adventures of a Wimpy Werewolf

I was convinced I'd been bitten by the dog, but by the time I got back there were only a few minor scratch marks on my back, and by the morning these had gone too.

I now see that I should have gone to the hospital, because I've contracted a very serious disease — rabies.

What else could it be? I've got rabies and now I'm going mad.

The earliest the doctor can see me is Tuesday. I can't wait that long! I'll be foaming at the mouth!

Oh God! I've just looked up rabies online and it says you can die within ten days of the first symptoms. That means I've got a week at best. I can't die! Who's going to lead this generation away from recklessness if I'm not around? I suppose Pete from the

21

Adventures of a Wimpy Werewolf

debating society could do it if the general public can learn to see past his uneven ears.

Friday 13TH April

I dread to imagine what bad luck this Friday the 13th will bring me. Maybe I should just stay in bed. No, I can't risk losing an entire day of school. My exams start in just two months' time. How did it all go so quickly?

I didn't have to wait long for the bad luck to start. I just looked in the bathroom mirror and saw that I'd somehow managed to grow a unibrow overnight. The patch

of skin between my eyebrows had sprouted thick hair, leaving me with a single gigantic brow that looked like Uncle Derek's moustache. I shaved a gap between my eyebrows, but when I caught my reflection in the hallway mirror a few minutes later I saw that it had grown right back again.

How am I supposed to get straight A stars in my GCSEs with a unibrow? The highest grade anyone with a unibrow could realistically expect would be a D.

Mum noticed I wasn't wearing my blazer this morning and asked if I'd be cold. It's fine, I'm sure my body will sprout a thick coat of hair or something.

Halfway through my history lesson this morning, I realized my mouth was open and my tongue was hanging out of the side. I think it was because I was hot, but I must have looked like one of those yokels whose jaw goes slack when they concentrate. I have to make sure this never happens again. I'm a rational prefect, not a brainless mouthbreather.

Adventures of a Wimpy Werewolf

We had a debating society meeting this lunchtime. The motion was 'This house would ban zoos', and Pete argued in favour of the motion while I argued against it. I usually look forward to debating society meetings, but I couldn't get into it today. I'd printed out a list of ten good reasons why zoos actually help animals, but when I read them out, they didn't seem convincing. After all, why should animals be cooped up in cages when they could be running around and chomping into prey?

Pete made a good point about how it was impossible to replicate the natural habitats of wild animals, and the three other members of the debating society applauded. He then folded his arms and smiled so smugly that all I wanted to do was slap him in the face.

I looked down at my hands and saw that my fingernails had hardened into sharp yellow claws. I shoved my hands into my pockets to hide them. Now I couldn't even check my notes, and needed to come up with something smart off the top of my head. The best thing I could think to say was that it was only his opinion and he was wrong so he should shut up.

It was without a doubt the weakest comeback in the history of the society. The motion was carried, and I skulked away with my hands still in my pockets.

Adventures of a Wimpy Werewolf

I turned up early for English this afternoon and sat at my usual desk at the front.

Then I had another funny turn. I started to worry that someone would come in and steal my desk. I felt like I needed to do something to mark that this was my desk, and no one else was allowed near it.

In a sort of daze, I stood up and... I'm not sure I can even bring myself to write this...

Okay, then. I stood up and did a wee around the desk. I honestly have no idea why I thought this was an appropriate thing to do.

As soon as I realized what I'd done, I grabbed a handful of paper towels from the toilets and mopped it up. Then I sprayed the whole classroom with Lynx and sat down again just as Mrs Nichols arrived.

Adventures of a Wimpy Werewolf

She complained about the deodorant and opened a window, but she didn't mention anything about urine, so I think I got away with it.

All this has got to stop. People have been locked up in mental homes for less.

Saturday 14TH April

I woke up at seven this morning and made myself a cup of coffee so I'd be ready to start revision at 7.15am as planned. According to my timetable, I was in for a busy morning of maths, followed by history, followed by English, followed by science, followed by an eighteen—minute lunch break.

But as I sat down and laid out my textbook, notebook and scientific calculator, the whole thing suddenly seemed like a massive waste of time. As the clouds parted and the sun shone through my window, I wondered why I was spending such a lovely day cooped up inside my room when I could be running around outside.

The rational part of my brain was horrified by this. I didn't spend an entire evening colour—coding my revision timetable so I could just ignore it and swan off on a whim. But another part of my mind reasoned that there were still a couple of months until exams, so what harm could it do?

Adventures of a Wimpy Werewolf

I stepped outside and ran down the street, expecting to get a stitch before the second lamp post. But to my surprise, I found myself running further and further, past the terraced houses, then the semi–detached ones, then the detached ones until I got to the fields to the north of town and eventually to Lunar Wood.

I ran round and round the wood all day, amazed at my stamina. I used to have trouble running for 400 metres, yet now I could sprint all day without flagging. I was so tired when I got home that I curled into a ball and went straight to sleep on my bedroom floor.

Adventures of a Wimpy Werewolf

Sunday 15TH April

I slept right through until morning after my spontaneous day of exercise. When I woke up my legs were so stiff that it took me ages just to walk to my desk.

I have now redrawn my timetable so that I can catch up with all the revision I planned to do yesterday. It's going to be tough, but I think I can cram it in.

Here goes.

That didn't work. I opened my maths textbook and tried to force myself to take it all in, but nothing happened. Then I tried with my science textbook, then my history textbook, then my French textbook. Still nothing.

After a while, I noticed some movement outside my window. There was a squirrel dashing up a tree outside my window. I stared at it as it darted around the trunk. For some reason, I found this utterly gripping. Anyone would think I was watching a *Doctor Who* season finale rather than a mangy rodent.

What's happening to me? Am I turning stupid? If so, can't my brain at least wait until I get my A star grades?

Mum went out for a drink with her friend Caroline tonight, leaving me to cook for myself. There was a lamb chop left in the fridge, so I got out a baking tray and turned the oven on.

But just as I was about to pop it in, I wondered why I needed to cook it at all. Wouldn't that take all the flavour out of it?

Without really knowing why, I bit off a chunk of the raw meat. To my surprise, it tasted fantastic. Why had I ever wanted to ruin the lovely meat by burning it and serving

it with mint sauce when it was perfect in its natural state?

By the time I'd finished, blood from the chop was running down my chin. I should have been ashamed of myself, but the meat was so lovely I didn't care.

I ran my tongue around my mouth and it felt like all my teeth had thickened and sharpened. But when I looked at them in the hallway mirror they seemed normal enough.

I was just woken up by some foxes rifling through our bins. Before I had time to think, I found myself running outside and growling at them. They darted off down the street, but I didn't see why I should let them get away with it. I ran after them, and was about to follow them into the back garden of number 42 when I stopped myself. Only a couple of months ago, I moved the debating society to tears with my impassioned anti-fox-hunting speech. Now I was engaging in the very activity I'd condemned. How quickly we betray our principles.

I'm going back to bed now and I'm not going to let the foxes bother me. They can have the litter if they want. I'm rising above it.

Adventures of a Wimpy Werewolf

Monday 16TH April

My body is determined to find new ways to embarrass me every day. In Science this morning, Mrs Marshall projected a diagram about atomic structure onto the whiteboard. I tried desperately to commit it to memory in case it came up in the exam, but it just wasn't sinking in.

As I strained and strained to make my brain remember it, something very unpleasant happened. I felt a warm shape forcing itself out at the back of my trousers.

Desperately hoping that no one else would notice me, I ran for the door and made straight for the toilets.

When I got there, I turned my back to the mirror and lifted up my shirt. It was more horrible than I could ever have imagined. At the top of my trousers there was a short, stubby tail wagging back and forth.

I reached around to touch the tail, but it shrank until I was looking at an ordinary human back again.

I returned to class, and faced the inevitable accusations that I'd had to run to the toilets because I'd had an accident in my trousers. The weird thing was, I was happy to let them think that, because the truth was worse.

31

Adventures of a Wimpy Werewolf

This has got to stop. I'm a prefect, for pity's sake.
I'm supposed to be setting an example. If other pupils
see prefects disrupting lessons, running around corridors
and growing tails, what's to stop them doing the same?
I just hope the doctor can give me some pills to make
this stop. I can't take much more.

I stopped by at Tesco on the way home and picked up
some steaks that had been reduced to £2.99. I was
planning to give them to Mum to cook for supper tonight,

but in the end I couldn't resist wolfing them down raw. I know I'm risking all sorts of weird diseases with this raw meat thing, but it was just too moreish. When I got back Mum offered to heat up some spaghetti hoops, so I told her I'd cook them myself later on.

I didn't, of course. Why should I bother with boring old tinned pasta when I could be eating delicious raw meat?

Tuesday 17TH April

Time for my appointment now. I'm usually nervous about going to the doctor in case he gives me an injection, but things have gone too far now. He can give me all the injections he likes if it makes my problems stop.

Adventures of a Wimpy Werewolf

I'm back from the doctor's now, and he's put me on a course of antibiotics.

To be perfectly honest, I don't think I did justice to the full horror of my situation. I wanted to tell him about my tail, but the memory of it disgusted me so much I couldn't speak. Then I tried to tell him about my upper body growing and shrinking, but he thought I was describing how it felt rather than what actually happened. Then I tried to tell him about my urge to wee around my desk and he suggested I might have a urinary tract infection, although I didn't have any of the other symptoms he listed.

In the end I came right out and said I thought I'd contracted rabies from a dog bite, but he wasn't convinced. He asked me how my general health was and I had to admit that I feel stronger and fitter than ever before.

He gave me an antibiotics prescription to get rid of me, but I haven't even bothered taking it to the chemists. Whatever's wrong with me, it's nothing that quack can help with.

Adventures of a Wimpy Werewolf

Wednesday 18TH April

Please stop this, body! Why are you doing this to me?

This morning I washed and conditioned my hair just as I always do.

As soon as I got to the school gates, Tyson and his gang started teasing me for having a mullet. I felt the back of my neck and there did indeed seem to be long hair covering it.

I ran into the toilets and looked at my reflection. For reasons best known to themselves, the hairs just above my neck had grown to shoulder length during my journey to school.

I left the house looking like an efficient prefect, and arrived at school looking like someone from the deep south of America whose mother is also his sister.

I grabbed a strong pair of scissors from the art stockroom and chopped the offensive locks off.

Please, hair, I'm begging you. Don't grow back. I just want an ordinary day. I need to get my head around simultaneous equations. I don't want to look like someone who still counts on their fingers.

Thursday 19TH April

The ginger cat from number 23 hissed and arched its back when I walked past this morning. I was rather surprised by this, because I've always got on quite well with it, and I've even stopped to stroke it once or twice.

I couldn't work out what I'd done to offend it at first, but then I remembered about the dream where I'd chased it through the forest. Could the cat somehow know about the dream? They are quite spooky, I suppose.

I walked over to the cat so I could show it I meant no harm, but it ran off down the street. But then I realized I did mean it harm. I wanted to catch it, pick it up with my teeth and shake it violently back and forth. Luckily, I managed to hold myself back from this idiotic behaviour before I got reported to an animal rights charity and became an international hate figure.

I got banned from the chess club this lunchtime. The very club I started over a year ago is now out of bounds to me. And the weird thing is, I don't even blame them.

I was paired up with Pete for the first game. I usually like to think three or four moves ahead when I'm playing, but today I couldn't even think of my next move. Every option I thought of seemed like it would lead to humiliating defeat, and the whole game began to annoy me. Why was I stuck in that stuffy classroom moving those little pieces around anyway?

My frustration grew, and without realizing what I was doing, I swiped all the pieces off the board and growled at Pete. When I looked down, I saw my nails had hardened into claws again. Karl and Roderick, who were playing next to us, looked across in disgust.

Adventures of a Wimpy Werewolf

I tried to apologize but Pete said my behaviour had gone against everything the chess club stood for. It was meant to be a haven from the usual brutish persecution of the gifted. He said I'd betrayed these principles and hit me with a lifetime ban.

I whimpered with shame and left the room.

Friday 20TH April

I saw a bus driving past as I left for school this morning, and decided to catch it so I could do some extra revision on the way in. Unfortunately, I just missed it. But rather than wait for the next one, I somehow thought it would be a good idea to chase the bus into school.

To my surprise, I almost caught up. I was focusing on it so intently I barely noticed how fast I was zooming along myself. It was only when I overtook a cyclist that I realized I must have been running at over twenty miles an hour. He gave me such an astonished look that I forced myself to stop and walk the rest of the way.

How did I get so good at running? When we did the 1500 metres race in PE, Mr Johnston let me stop after the third lap as everyone else had already finished.

By the time I got to the history classroom I was streaming with sweat. The only seat left was on a table with Erica, Julia and Amanda, the most attractive girls in Year Eleven. I usually avoid sitting with them, because they make me so nervous I can't concentrate, but today I had no choice.

At first I felt very self-conscious about how I smelt after all that running, but then I began to feel strangely proud. I put my hands behind my head, letting the reek from my armpits out.

Erica, Julia and Amanda looked at each other and winced. I should have been ashamed, but I wasn't. They were the ones who were in the wrong. They were the ones who covered up their natural odour with body mist and roll—on deodorant, while I let mine flood into their snouts.

I lurched violently forward in my chair, slamming my head into the desk. Under the table, my legs had cracked into painful haunches, with every muscle, bone and vein agonizingly stretched. A few seconds later, they shrank back, flinging me back upright.

This sent the class into a fit of shame coughs, so I stared at my textbook, pretending to get on with my work.

The class soon lost interest and returned to their own conversations. I patted my legs under the desk and found they were completely bare. Whatever had happened to them, it had ripped off my school trousers, leaving just my stretchy nylon briefs intact. Thank God I didn't wear boxer shorts to be cool. I doubt they'd have survived. I picked the fragments of polyester off the floor and arranged them over my thighs into a semblance of trousers.

At the end of the lesson I waited for everyone to leave the room and sneaked out into the corridor, holding my satchel in front of me. I had to think fast. I was tiptoeing down the corridor outside the history room with just my shirt and underpants on. If anyone spotted me, this was going straight onto YouTube. I'd be known as 'no—trousers boy' for the rest of my life

and I'd never be able to
leave the house again.
  I heard the door
at the end of the
corridor creaking open.
With nowhere else to
go, I dashed into the
cleaner's cupboard.

It's now 8pm and I've just
got back home. I waited
until I was absolutely sure
the caretaker had gone
and then I ran down to the
PE changing rooms. I grabbed a pair of black shorts
from the spare kit box, opened the fire escape doors
and ran straight back here.
  How can I ever go back to school knowing that my
clothes could fly off my body at any time?

41

Adventures of a Wimpy Werewolf

Saturday 21ST April

Today I went down to the shopping precinct to buy some baggy clothes. I thought that if I bought the largest shirts and trousers I could find, they might survive any further freaky expanding my body chose to do.

At first I tried the school uniform section of Marks & Spencer, but even the largest sizes looked like they'd rip apart.

In the end, I went to JJB Sports and bought a huge pair of elasticated tracksuit bottoms and a hooded top with roomy sleeves. I could expand to the size of a family car without breaking those.

I know I'll be flouting school uniform rules for the first time with this new outfit, but if I don't wear it I could end up naked in class. And that's not just against school rules, it's against the law.

Sunday 22ND April

I jumped with fright at the sight of my reflection in the bathroom mirror this morning. My eyes had turned bright yellow, and the pupils had elongated into dark vertical slits.

Adventures of a Wimpy Werewolf

I blinked, and my eyes returned to their usual pale blue. I had no idea if this was just another hallucination, but I couldn't take any chances. I rooted around in my drawer for my sunglasses and put them on. Luckily, it's a nice day, so they won't look too out of place.

Mum just asked what was behind my new image. I said she wouldn't understand so she teased me about being a moody teenager.

I wanted to tell her all about the funny turns I've been having, but all that came out was a grunt.

Then she said I must have bought new clothes to impress a girl and asked me if I had a girlfriend. I ran upstairs to my room, which she took as evidence that she'd guessed right. I don't know why this made her so pleased. You'd think with her dating history she wouldn't want to see me set off on that rocky road.

I went into Tesco just before closing time and found they had loads of reduced meat. I got a massive bagful for under a tenner, including pork chops, lamb cutlets and steaks, and I tucked into it on the way home.

Adventures of a Wimpy Werewolf

Now I'm completely stuffed and I've still got some left over for lunch tomorrow. I know I should put it in the fridge, but I somehow feel as if it won't be fully safe unless I keep it right next to me all night.

Monday 23RD April

I was late for school again this morning because I was distracted by a smell. I was just turning the corner of my street, when I detected an odour and felt compelled to investigate it. I got down on my hands and knees so I could track the scent with greater accuracy.

It ended up leading me to a squirrel that was climbing

an oak tree in someone's garden. I wasn't sure what I was supposed to do now I'd tracked it, so I got back on my feet and walked to school.

I don't know what I expected to find that was so exciting. An invisibility ring? A lightsaber? A sonic screwdriver? At any rate, I need to stop myself from getting misled by silly smells from now on.

We all had to pair up to conduct an experiment in science this morning. I usually choose Pete, but by the time I got there he was already sitting next to a boy with thick glasses called Roger. The only person left was Amanda, one of the girls who'd caused my trousers to fly off on Friday. I was worried this might happen again, so I avoided speaking to her as she set up the Bunsen burner, tripod and boiling tube. But when she asked about what had happened last week, I thought it would be rude to ignore her. I told her that I'd been ill, but I was feeling much better now.

After that, we started chatting and I found that she was much friendlier when she wasn't with Erica and Julia. I kept checking my hands and legs for hairs, but nothing seemed to be happening, so I thought I might be okay for once.

Adventures of a Wimpy Werewolf

After a few minutes, Amanda said I had something on the back of my trousers. I felt around the back of them, and found that my tail had grown back. And this time, rather than a small stump, I'd sprouted a large, bushy tail that went almost down to my knees.

I turned to face Amanda, so she couldn't see it. But she was determined to find out what it was, and tried to turn me around. I was strong enough to resist her, but

unfortunately the physical contact made my tail wag vigorously back and forth behind me.

My tail knocked over the tripod and Bunsen burner and sent the boiling tube crashing to the floor. I stuffed it up the back of my shirt and tried to pick everything up, but it was too late. The class had erupted into a chorus of shame coughs and Mrs Marshall sent me out for disrupting the lesson.

At lunchtime, I went behind the playground bins to enjoy the rest of my meat bag. You might not think the scummy area behind the wheelie bins is an especially nice place to go for lunch, but when you're addicted to raw meat your standards of mealtime ambience fall sharply.

After that, I took my Ribena carton along to the canteen to keep up a pretence of normality. But by the time I'd got there, Roger had taken my usual place next to Pete, Karl and Roderick.

I didn't want them to see me sitting on my own, so I went over to Tyson's gang instead. They weren't especially welcoming, and asked if I was drinking carrot juice or ginger beer, even though it was clear from the carton that the drink was blackcurrant—flavoured. The irony is that I quite like carrot juice and ginger beer, but I wouldn't dream of drinking them in school for fear of giving them ammunition.

While I was with Tyson, I thought I might as well remind him that he's still got my copy of *Grand Theft Auto*, but he just shrugged and said he hadn't finished it yet. I lent it to him in January. How long is he going to take? The worst thing is, I can't even go to the police about it because it's rated 18, so they'd probably send me to prison for buying it in the first place.

Mr Landis called me into his office as I was leaving school.

At first he looked at me in silence and shook his head. Then he said he'd seen it all before — hardworking, well-behaved pupils getting led astray by the cool kids.

He said that since the day my blazer was ripped I'd been disobeying school uniform rules and wearing cool gear like hoodies and dark glasses instead. Now he was getting reports about me turning up late, getting thrown out of lessons and hanging around with Tyson's gang instead of the respectable pupils like Pete and Karl.

He said that I could go on following Tyson and his

little entourage right to the unemployment office after school if I liked. Then I'd see how cool they were.

I wanted to tell him my new clothes were down to a medical condition, but when I tried to speak, all that came out was a high-pitched yapping noise.

He walked over to his door and opened it for me. He said that if I wasn't taking my future seriously, he didn't see why he should.

Adventures of a Wimpy Werewolf

Tonight I thought about how Tyson had stolen my copy of *Grand Theft Auto*, and it made me really angry. What right did he have to steal my property?

I could hear a strange noise in my bedroom and for a moment I couldn't work out what it was. Then I realized that it was me. I was growling. I stopped right away, and tried to get back to my science textbook.

But I kept glancing over at my games collection and worrying that Tyson would come round and steal those too. For some reason, I decided that the only way I could make absolutely sure they were safe would be to bury them in the back garden.

I took the shovel out of the shed, dug a hole and threw my all my PS3 games into it. I knew the damp soil would damage the packaging of the games, and send their exchange value plummeting, but I somehow felt they'd be safer this way.

Just as I was finishing, Mum popped her head out of the kitchen window and asked me

what I was doing. I was too tired to lie, so I told her I was burying my computer games to make sure they were safe.

She said that she now realized I couldn't possibly have a girlfriend after all. For some reason, this put her in a bad mood for the rest of the night. I don't know why she's still so convinced that romance is the answer to everything. She's had three boyfriends since Dad left and they've all been complete losers. And that's coming from someone who's just buried their copy of *street Fighter IV* in the back garden.

Tuesday 24TH April

According to my revision timetable, I should be waking up at six every morning this week to fit in an extra hour of study before school. As a matter of fact, I did wake up early today, but opening my textbooks was the last thing I felt like.

I felt like I needed to get outside and release all the energy that was pent up inside me. I didn't plan my route, but I found myself heading out to the fields to the north of Newchester again and making for Lunar Wood.

It was so early that I had the woods pretty much to myself. The only other jogger was an older teenager with short ginger hair and a white vest.

Adventures of a Wimpy Werewolf

He was running the opposite way around the track, and smiled at me when we passed, as if he recognized me. I was pretty sure I've never seen him before. He looked really tough, and had loads of strange tattoos up the side of his arms with pictures of moons and slogans like 'No surrender' and 'Support our troops'. He doesn't look like the sort of person I'd make friends with.

Adventures of a Wimpy Werewolf

On my second lap of the wood, I had another of my funny turns. This time my whole body bloated out, and I threw myself down to the ground. I felt like all my muscles were twisting and tearing apart and my bones were breaking and reforming over and over again.

A few seconds later, it was all over. I stood up, brushed off the dirt and looked at the damage. My baggy tracksuit bottoms and hoodie had survived the stretching, thank God. The only casualties were my shoes, which had split into useless scraps of leather and rubber. But that's all right. I'll just wear my trainers with the laces really loose, so they'll slip off rather than rip apart next time.

I made my way out of the woods and back across the fields towards Newchester. After a few minutes I saw the jogger coming after me, so I tried to speed up in case he'd seen my funny turn. But it was difficult to run across the uneven ground with no shoes on, and he caught up easily.

He handed me the ruptured remains of my shoes and I thanked him. Then he asked why I'd howled, and I said it must have been someone else.

The jogger stared at me in silence for a couple of minutes. Then he said he knew what I was going through and he could help.

I should have begged him to tell me what he knew. But

Adventures of a Wimpy Werewolf

I was so freaked out by the notion that he might have seen me that I turned and ran away.

This time he didn't follow. He just shouted after me that it was up to me to decide if I wanted help, but if I did, I should email him at RYANSAVAGE1987@HOTMAIL.COM

By the time I got home it was too late to go to school, so I sneaked back into my room and pulled the covers over my head.

I won't take this Ryan guy up on his offer. I think he's probably from a religious cult. He heard my cry of anguish and decided to exploit my weakness and recruit me. I'll forget I ever met him.

Wednesday 25TH April

I have now resolved to forget all about my illness and go back to normal. Whatever condition I've got, it's surely just a case of mind over matter. If I stay focused and confident, I'll no doubt be able to behave like a normal person and get my life back on track.

Adventures of a Wimpy Werewolf

It all seems to be working so far, touch wood. I sat through Maths this morning without humiliating myself in a bizarre way. It's lunchtime now and I'm reading my history textbook on a bench in the playground. I'm still alarmingly behind with everything, but I've had a decent morning for once. I might even reward myself by joining in the game of football on the playing field.

The football players were very reluctant to let me join in at first, and I could hardly blame them. Whenever I'd been forced to play in PE, I'd usually passed the lesson at the side of the pitch talking to Pete about *Doctor Who*. But this time I really wanted to play, and eventually they gave in.

I think they were quite surprised by my energy as I bounded around after the ball. I didn't really get a touch, but I was enjoying the exercise nonetheless.

After about ten minutes, I got my big chance. The ball rolled towards my feet just a few metres from goal. Surely, I'd be able to tap it in and taste sporting glory for the first time in my life.

I can't remember why I did this, but I got down on my hands and knees and picked up the ball with my teeth.

Adventures of a Wimpy Werewolf

Then I trotted over to the goalkeeper and spat it at his feet.

Everyone stopped playing and waited for me to leave the pitch. The other members of my team shouted things like 'Mouthball!' as I shamefully made my way off the field. I noticed the ball had now rolled past the feet of the keeper and into the net, and was going to suggest they count it as a goal, but I thought I'd better leave them to it.

I'm back home now, and getting on with my science revision. I'm trying not to think about the match. It doesn't really matter. I was never friends with the football gang anyway. It's not like I showed myself up in front of anyone I liked.

Thursday 26TH April

I noticed the squashed remains of a squirrel on my way in this morning. I can't usually look at things like that, but this morning I found myself drawn to it. It couldn't have been dead for more than a few minutes, and it smelt so fresh it made my mouth water. I got down on my hands and knees and took a whiff. I

wondered why I should let this lovely meat go rotten on the side of road when I could pop it in my mouth and enjoy its succulent flavour.

I think I would have actually done so if an

Adventures of a Wimpy Werewolf

old lady hadn't shouted at me. She accused me of being on drugs and threatened to make a citizen's arrest and march me down to the police station. I pretended I'd dropped my contact lens, but she wasn't convinced.

Then I ran off to Tesco and bought some reduced chicken drumsticks to eat on the way in. Chewing raw meat off the bone might be pretty scuzzy, but if it stops me lapping up roadkill, it's what I'll have to do.

When I got into my science lesson, Mrs Marshall was handing out multiple-choice tests to check how our revision was coming along. Apparently she'd announced this on Tuesday while I was away.

I felt my heart beating quicker in my chest as she placed my paper in front of me. I was going to ask to be excused, but I got a decent amount of revision done last night, so I thought I might as well give it a try.

I turned over the sheet and glanced through the questions. I could answer them. This was going to be fine.

I tried to pick up my pen but it fell out of my grasp and rolled along the desk. I looked down at my hands. The thick hairs had returned, but this time something even odder had happened. The lower half of my hands had stretched to twice their normal length, and my thumb and fingers were now a few inches apart.

For a while, I managed to grip the pen between my middle finger and my index finger. But then my fingers shrank into hairy stumps and it fell away again.

Adventures of a Wimpy Werewolf

I shoved my paws into my armpits, staring at the paper in frustration. I glanced around the room. Everyone was concentrating too hard on their papers to worry about me, so I grabbed the pen with my teeth and circled the correct options.

My claws were digging into my underarms and blood was trickling down my sleeves, but I went on anyway, determined to complete the paper.

After a couple of minutes of this, Mrs Marshall shouted at me to take the exam more seriously. She said that I might find it easy, but that was no reason to mess around while others were concentrating. I dropped the pen and sat back in my chair, staring helplessly at the questions I knew the answers to.

At the end of the lesson, Mrs Marshall came round to collect our papers and I noticed that my hands had returned to normal. I tried to circle as many answers as I could before she reached my desk, but I didn't get far.

I dread to think how I've done. There was a pupil at my old school who actually scored less than 25 per cent on a multiple-choice science exam with four options for each question. I tried to explain to him how statistically unlikely this was, but he'd failed maths too so he didn't understand. I don't think I've done as badly as that, but I can't be far off.

Adventures of a Wimpy Werewolf

At lunchtime I decided to go round to Mr Landis' office to apologize for my behaviour on Monday. I wanted him to know that I still took my responsibilities as a prefect seriously, even though I'd let myself down by barking at him. I intended to assure him that

my behaviour was brought on by a fit of exam stress, and it wouldn't happen again.

When I got to the office, I somehow took it upon myself to whimper and pat the door with my hands instead of knocking. As soon as I realized what I was doing, I blushed with shame and dashed off down the corridor. Unfortunately, Mr Landis stuck his head out just in time to see me running around the corner. He told me I'd get a whole week of detention if he caught me playing such stupid pranks again.

This can't go on any longer. I want to email that Ryan guy, but what can I write? I can hardly ask him if he has any advice about stopping your hands from turning into paws. He'll report me to the loony bin.

Friday 27TH April

Today Mr Landis called everyone from Year Eleven into the assembly hall to lecture us on how important our exams are. I think it was meant to motivate the lazy kids, but as I'm already well aware of how much is riding on the upcoming examinations, it sent me into a fluster.

I thought about how far behind I was with my revision and how few hours there were between now and my first exam on June 16th. I wondered if I should try to stay awake until then.

I thought about how my hands had deformed during the science test. What if that happened in my real exams? What if I failed them all?

I tried to tell Mr Landis to stop freaking me out. I

wanted him to let me go and get on with my work right away. But all that came out when I opened my mouth was a terrified howl.

Everyone in the assembly hall broke into laughter and Mr Landis stopped mid-rant. He pointed at the exit and told me to leave. He said that I wouldn't find it a laughing matter when I failed my exams. I want to tell him that I was already aware of this and he was just making it worse, but I didn't want to speak in case a moo or a miaow came out this time.

Adventures of a Wimpy Werewolf

As I trudged out to the sound of shame coughs, Mr Landis shook his head and said he expected better from a prefect and that I'd let myself down.

I know I've let myself down. That's about all I do know at the moment. I don't know what's happening to me, I don't know how to stop it and I don't know what career options are open to someone with all the communication skills of Lassie, but I know I've let myself down.

Saturday 28TH April

Okay, I've got to do this. I've got to contact Ryan. So what if he wants to brainwash me? I've got to talk to someone. And so far, he's the only person who's offered to help.

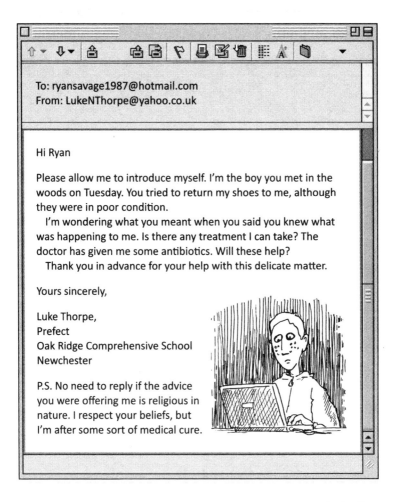

To: ryansavage1987@hotmail.com
From: LukeNThorpe@yahoo.co.uk

Hi Ryan

Please allow me to introduce myself. I'm the boy you met in the woods on Tuesday. You tried to return my shoes to me, although they were in poor condition.

I'm wondering what you meant when you said you knew what was happening to me. Is there any treatment I can take? The doctor has given me some antibiotics. Will these help?

Thank you in advance for your help with this delicate matter.

Yours sincerely,

Luke Thorpe,
Prefect
Oak Ridge Comprehensive School
Newchester

P.S. No need to reply if the advice you were offering me is religious in nature. I respect your beliefs, but I'm after some sort of medical cure.

I sent the email and then spent the whole afternoon staring at my inbox and clicking the 'refresh' icon. I know I should have been revising, but I was too curious about what he'd say.

Adventures of a Wimpy Werewolf

It wasn't until four hours later that I got a reply.

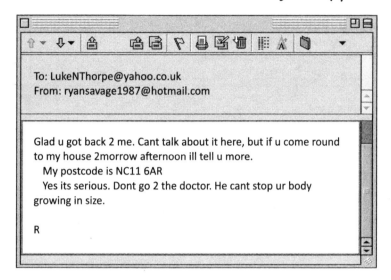

To: LukeNThorpe@yahoo.co.uk
From: ryansavage1987@hotmail.com

Glad u got back 2 me. Cant talk about it here, but if u come round to my house 2morrow afternoon ill tell u more.
   My postcode is NC11 6AR
   Yes its serious. Dont go 2 the doctor. He cant stop ur body growing in size.

R

My first instinct was to delete the email and forget I'd ever contacted him. I'm not in the practice of turning up at the houses of strangers, especially those who can't spell. I mean, how much time does it actually save to type the number 2 rather than the letters 't' and 'o'? How could this illiterate man possibly know more about my condition than a doctor?

I wondered if it was all a scam to get me round to his house so he could steal my phone and bankcard. But when I got to the bit about my body growing in size, I started to think that this guy might actually know something useful to me.

Adventures of a Wimpy Werewolf

I googled the postcode, expecting to find it was in the middle of a rough estate. Surprisingly, the map was showing me a detached house near the woods where I'd seen him jogging.

Surely he couldn't be too hard up for money if he lived in a country mansion? I doubted he'd be interested in my battered Nokia or my £86.42 savings.

Adventures of a Wimpy Werewolf

To: ryansavage1987@hotmail.com
From: LukeNThorpe@yahoo.co.uk

Hi Ryan

Thank you so much for your prompt reply. I shall call round at your house at 2pm tomorrow. Hope this is acceptable.

I look forward to our meeting.

Yours sincerely,

Luke Thorpe

I feel quite hopeful now. Ideally, I'll turn up at Ryan's house tomorrow, he'll give me some medicine, my erratic behaviour will cease and I'll be back to my revision by late afternoon.

Sunday 29TH April

Ryan's house turned out to be a large manor house on a hill overlooking Lunar Woods. There was no signpost or address at the end of the driveway, but it was the only house on the lane, so I thought it must be the right one.

Ten windows faced out across the top floor, while eight windows and an elaborate porch stretched across the bottom floor. There was even an annexe on the side that must have been for servants once. I wondered how a teenager with bad spelling could possibly live in such a place. Did he have rich parents? Was he a rapper? A footballer?

Adventures of a Wimpy Werewolf

As I got closer, I noticed how run—down the place looked. Several of the windows were broken, and a loose tile slid off the roof and smashed on the driveway as I approached. The words 'Lunar Hall' were etched above the doorway on cracked stone.

Maybe Ryan was part of some criminal gang. Maybe he was going to talk me into smuggling drugs. I stopped, wondering if I should go any further. But then Ryan appeared in the doorway and beckoned me in.

Inside, the house looked even more decrepit and run—down. Huge chunks of plaster had been gouged from the walls, and the bare floorboards were covered with countless scratches. The whole place stunk of moulting hairs and rotten meat, and there were burst footballs and dirty tennis balls in every corner.

I asked Ryan what he knew about my condition, but he said he'd have to show me rather than tell me, and led me into a room that contained nothing except a few circular bits of metal attached to the wall.

I began to feel very uncomfortable. I told Ryan I'd made a mistake and I needed to go, but he blocked the exit. I tried to shove him out of the way, but he pushed me back to the wall. I struggled against him, but it was no use. He yanked my wrists up and fastened them into the steel manacles on the wall. I tried to pull against the shackles, but they held fast.

I'd been nervous about visiting Ryan, but it turned out the truth was worse than I could possibly have imagined. He wasn't a footballer. He wasn't a rapper. He wasn't even a robber. He was a serial killer. And now he'd lured me to this deserted house to kill me.

I couldn't believe I was going to be killed! It would be in all the papers! And the only photo Mum would give them would be that embarrassing one of me performing magic tricks at my thirteenth birthday party. She's always loved that picture. I have no idea why.

Ryan walked out and I tried to shout for help, but all that came out was a piercing howl. I felt like I was having another of my funny turns, where my body expands and my bones crack into weird shapes, though I was so terrified I didn't really know what was going on.

I could hear Ryan stomping back down the corridor. Oh God, what was he going to bring? A knife? A gun? A chainsaw?

Ryan walked in carrying a mirror. Except it couldn't have been a mirror, because when he held it up to my face, I saw a large ginger dog. Except that wasn't quite right either. It wasn't a dog at all. It was a wolf.

A few minutes later, I felt myself shrink down again and my howl turned back into a scream. This turned into confused sobbing as I tried to make sense of what had happened.

It must have been an hour before I could speak again. The first question I asked Ryan was how he'd known. Instead of replying, he rolled his hands into fists and looked up at the ceiling with intense concentration until the veins on his neck bulged into thick tubes and a pelt of ginger fur burst out of his skin. He roared until his jaw jutted forward into a muzzle. Then he spread out his hands and howled as his ribcage wrenched itself apart. His legs hunched and twisted beneath his jogging bottoms and his feet arched into paws.

Adventures of a Wimpy Werewolf

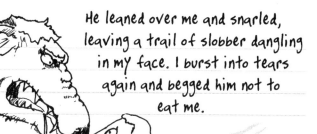

He leaned over me and snarled, leaving a trail of slobber dangling in my face. I burst into tears again and begged him not to eat me.

I'm a werewolf. A wolfman. A lycanthrope. A shape-shifter. No matter how I put it, it doesn't make sense. But I can hardly deny it now, can I?

After Ryan turned human again, he undid my shackles and patiently answered my questions about the condition. It was a bit like that time Mr Landis outlined my duties as a prefect. Except that it involved transforming into a bloodthirsty supernatural beast rather than reporting people for running in the corridors.

It turns out that Ryan is actually twenty-five years old. He looks younger because you age much slower when you're a wolfman. He says that most werewolves live until over 150, which is a bonus. I wonder if I'll live to see those hovering skateboards out of *Back to the Future 2*.

The only things that might prevent you living so

Adventures of a Wimpy Werewolf

long are silver bullets, which are fatal, and a flower called wolfsbane, which can paralyse you long enough for someone to chop you up. But an enemy would have to know you were a werewolf to use either of these, so you're safe as long as you keep a low profile.

I don't suppose that growing a tail in a science lesson counts as keeping a low profile, though I doubt any of my classmates want to be werewolf slayers. I certainly can't remember anyone mentioning it that time the careers guidance officer visited.

Ryan said he was transformed into a wolf when he was bitten at the age of thirteen. He says that most wolves are transformed by bites, although it's possible you can inherit the condition if both your parents have it.

Adventures of a Wimpy Werewolf

I told him about the night I was bitten and he said it was probably one of the wolves from his pack. Although he does his best to keep them under control during full moons, there are occasions when a wolf strays and bites someone. I thought he might apologize for this oversight, but he didn't. I think he sees the condition as a privilege rather than a curse anyway.

Then I told him about the night I trashed my room and he said this was typical of a first transformation. It often throws your mind into such a state of confusion that you can't remember anything afterwards. Most wolfpeople get better at remembering their lupine state as time goes on, though some never manage it.

Since my first transformation, I've been experiencing involuntary partial changes brought about by excitement or panic. Ryan said he was sorry he had to frighten me to bring on another full change, but it was the only way he could show me the truth.

I then asked him why I didn't have to wait until the full moon to transform, like the werewolves you see on TV. And here's the cool bit. Apparently, most werewolves only transform on the three nights around the full moon, but there is a much rarer type called 'alpha wolves', who can transform at any time, and I'm one of those. Ryan is also one, which is why he is pack leader.

Although I don't have control over my changes yet, I'll

Adventures of a Wimpy Werewolf

be able to turn them on and off as I get used to them. Ryan then offered to mentor me in wolf skills, and I thanked him, but said that I should wait until after my GCSEs so I can focus on it properly.

In the meantime, I've agreed to join Ryan's pack, which is called the Lunar Wood Pack. Apparently, it's one of the oldest in the country, and draws wolves from as far afield as Burnton and Stockfield every full moon.

I can't believe I'm going to meet them all the week after next. Ryan reckons they'll be overjoyed about getting a new alpha wolf. Although that's exactly how Mr Landis said the school would feel about getting a new prefect, and that turned out to be a big fat lie.

I hope this doesn't mean I can't become a politician now. I don't see why it should. As long as election night doesn't fall on a full moon, I should be able to balance wolf life with a political career. Having said that, the tabloids would have a field day if I ate someone

live on *Question Time*. You'd need a good PR guy to put a positive spin on that.

Monday 30TH April

Part of me thinks I should forget my exams and go back to Ryan's house for training this week, but they're so close now I really want to get them out of the way first. It's much easier to get things done if you focus on them one at a time. Memorize the periodic table today; master shape-shifting tomorrow. That kind of thing.

Anyway, I'm sure I'll be able to control my body a lot easier now I know more about my condition. Ryan said that stress and panic are the things that make me transform, so as long as I keep calm, I should be able to make it through the day without supernatural incident.

Today was a lot better. I started to get nervous in History when Mr Jordan went through all the topics that might come up on the exam, and I spotted thick ginger hairs pushing up through my skin again. But then I took deep breaths until my hand went back to normal. It wasn't so difficult. If Luke Skywalker can defeat the

Adventures of a Wimpy Werewolf

Galactic Empire and restore freedom to the galaxy, I'm sure I can stop a few silly hairs from growing. Although I must admit I identify more with Chewbacca than my namesake these days.

Tuesday 1ˢᵀ May

Okay, perhaps I was a little premature when I said I had full control over my body. We got our exam papers back in science today and I got an E. How can I have dropped from an A star to an E since Christmas? Surely no one in the history of GCSEs has ever descended from genius to dunce so quickly.

I saw the wolf hairs coming through on my hands again and tried to take deep breaths, but this time it didn't work. I just kept thinking about the humiliation of opening my exam results and seeing the letter 'E' next to every subject. The best job you can get with qualifications like that is asking people if you can return their shopping trolleys and keep the pound deposit.

I felt the vertebrae on my back popping up one by one and realized the whole wolf thing was going to happen, and the best course of action open to me now was to hide.

I padded into the corridor and made for the

78

cleaners' supply cupboard. I threw myself in and slammed the door shut. After a few seconds of the familiar stretching pain, I was in wolf form again. My head was almost touching the ceiling of the tiny room, and my tail was knocking bottles of floor cleaner off the shelves as it wagged behind me.

Now I was in full wolf form, I didn't want to hide at all. I wanted to leap out into the playground and chomp some throat.

Adventures of a Wimpy Werewolf

I can't believe I wanted to commit brutal murder! I had a sleepless night with guilt that time I sneaked onto the train without buying a ticket! Yet now I was ravenous for an unlimited buffet of Year Seven pupils. What have I become?

Luckily, I was too stupid to work out how to open the door when I was in wolf form. I flailed around at the handle for ages, but with an IQ in single figures and no opposable thumbs it was too much for me.

It's weird how stupid I get when I switch into wolf form. I might try it next time Mum makes me sit through her *Mamma Mia!* DVD.

As soon as I was human again, I did my best to put all the cleaning bottles back on the shelves and skulked off down the corridor.

I passed Mr Landis as I was leaving the building, and he tutted at me. He said that I was trying so hard to be one of the tough kids I'd even adopted the 'bad boy limp', which is this walk Tyson's gang do when they drag one of their legs behind them. I looked down and saw that one of my legs was still in wolf form.

I've just downloaded a relaxation course to my iPod. If

Adventures of a Wimpy Werewolf

I feel another transformation coming on, I can just pop my headphones on and calm down again.

Wednesday 2ND May

I stopped off at Tesco this morning to get another meat bag. There wasn't any meat in the reduced section so I had to make do with value sausages. I used to get squeamish about eating cheap sausages because every time I chewed a hard bit, I'd imagine it was a lip or an eyelid, but it doesn't bother me any more. Once you've experienced an overwhelming hunger to chew out an Adam's apple, eating a pig's eyelid is no big deal.

I was just about to sneak behind the wheelie bins and eat them when I was hit full in the face by a football. I turned round, expecting

Adventures of a Wimpy Werewolf

someone to apologize, but instead I saw Tyson and his friends laughing. He said he'd been expecting me to catch it in my mouth and drop it off at his feet.

I tried to ignore him, but it didn't work. I could feel my nails sharpening as my feet morphed into paws. I flung myself behind the bins and frantically rooted around for my iPod.

I grabbed it from the bottom of my bag, glad that I'd spent the extra £2.99 on a screen protector now that I was handling it with sharp, lupine claws. I stuck the earbuds in and clicked on my relaxation course, even as my fingers were shrinking into stubs.

I could hear whale song and an American woman telling me I was walking through a forest to a beautiful waterfall. Unfortunately, this was all I heard. My headphones popped out onto the floor as my ears migrated to the top of my head. It was too late. I was no longer the species MP3 players are designed for.

I threw myself down to the ground, hoping that the wheelie bins would shield me from sight. The last thing I wanted was for all the pupils to notice that there was a werewolf in the school grounds. They were excited enough that time a dog ran in.

I think I must have stayed in wolf form for three or four minutes. I can remember my wolf mode much more clearly now. My stomach aches with hunger and my

Adventures of a Wimpy Werewolf

thoughts become sluggish and confused like that New Year's Eve when I tried some of Mum's Baileys. Smell becomes more important than sight and I'm instantly aware of hundreds of pungent aroma trails.

The part of my brain that was still human told me to stay behind the bins and keep out of sight before someone called the silver bullet division of Rentokil. But the wolf part of my brain just wanted to get out there and feed. I knew it was wrong, but I couldn't stop myself. It was a bit like that time I ate that whole packet of Jaffa Cakes I was meant to be emptying into the biscuit tin.

Just as I was about to pounce out, I shrank back into human form. I wiped the dust from my tracksuit, and stepped back into the playground. A Year Nine boy ran past shouting, 'Freckle head!' He'd probably have kept quiet if he'd known just how close he came to being lunch.

This urge I have to eat humans is wrong. In fact, it's pretty much the definition of 'wrong'. There are lots of impulsive urges that people will be happy to help you overcome, but hunger for human flesh isn't one of them. I'm pretty sure the school counselor doesn't have a leaflet called 'So you're thinking about cannibalism?'

Adventures of a Wimpy Werewolf

Thursday 3RD May

We break up for study leave tomorrow, so we're having a school trip to Alton Towers today as a treat. Last time we went there, I spent most of the day wandering around the gardens because I was too frightened to go on the rides. But this year I'm going to give them a go. They can hardly be any more scary than turning into a throat-munching beast, can they?

On second thoughts, going to a theme park in my present condition wasn't such a smart idea.

I was having a very enjoyable day at first. I resisted sticking my head out of the coach window on the way there, even though I reckoned the wind would feel good on my face. I'm also pleased to say I resisted joining in when Tyson flicked the Vs at a passing coach of old people. He threatened anyone who didn't join in with a dead arm, but I ignored him. I already have my insatiable desire for human flesh on my conscience. I don't want to have upsetting elderly people on there too.

When we got into the theme park, I followed my classmates onto the log flume and river rapids, which

Adventures of a Wimpy Werewolf

were enjoyable enough. But then Tyson said we should all go on Nemesis before there was a queue. Erica and Amanda opted out, which is exactly what I should have done.

I got on the ride, pulled the safety harness down over my shoulders and strapped it to the chair. It certainly seemed secure enough.

As soon as the ride set off I knew I'd made a mistake. The metal rails flung us around blind corners, hurtling us up to the sky one minute and down to the ground the next. I tried to calm myself down, but a speeding rollercoaster isn't exactly the place for breathing exercises.

Adventures of a Wimpy Werewolf

On the final bend, it finally proved too much. My upper body doubled in size, ripping the safety harness off. I was flung twenty feet up in the air and splatted into a tree.

I thudded down to the floor and got back on my feet. I was now in a quiet wooded area of the park and I'm ashamed to admit I was feeling peckish for throat again. Despite the park's excellent range of takeaway options, I had a hunger that could only be satisfied by human prey.

I growled at a group of passing teenagers. They didn't seem very scared, although one of the girls said I was more convincing than the Frankenstein.

A few minutes later, I snapped back to human form again and looked around. The area I'd been walking around was called 'Horror Hollow', and it featured a man dressed as Frankenstein's monster discussing football with a man dressed as a zombie. On the bench behind them, there was a man in a werewolf costume reading a copy of the *Sun*. I was quite pleased I'd been able to cover for someone taking a break, although I doubt he'd have thanked me if I'd eaten those teenagers and he'd been arrested for it.

When I found my classmates, they were surprised that I was unharmed and said I should sue the park for their faulty safety equipment. None of them mentioned

Adventures of a Wimpy Werewolf

anything about huge flying wolves, so I think I got away with it again.

Friday 4TH May

I know I shouldn't really go back to school while I'm experiencing these violent urges, but today is the last full day of lessons before study leave, so I can't really miss it.

As long as I keep my head down and spend lunchtime in the library, I'm sure I can avoid getting nervous or angry and turning wolf.

Whoops. I did a pretty good job of focusing on my work for most of the day. I even waited for everyone to leave after the final lesson. But just as I was walking out of the gates, I saw that Tyson was still hanging around outside.

He shouted 'Gingernut' at me as I walked past. It wasn't a very cutting insult, and I've heard it hundreds of times before, but it still managed to wind me up.

I'm a werewolf, I thought. I have superior strength and speed, and yet this feeble human thinks he's got the right to mock me. I tried to control myself, but

Adventures of a Wimpy Werewolf

it was no use. I ran back towards Tyson as my hand expanded into a paw and then I struck him on the back of the head, knocking him to the ground.

I hid my paw behind my back as Tyson looked up at me with astonishment. I tried to pretend I'd been swatting a wasp, but it was no use. He got to his feet again and strode towards me with blood trickling down his neck.

Anyone else would have been frightened about what he'd do to them, but I was more frightened about what I'd do to him. The coppery smell of his blood hit my nostrils and I wanted nothing more than to lap it up.

I could feel hairs pushing through my skin and I

needed to get away. I ran as fast as I could, pushing my legs forward even as they stretched into haunches. As soon as I was around the corner, I threw myself into the bin of school dinner scraps. Just as I'd hoped, the rotten smells distracted me as I transformed into full wolf form and I quickly forgot all about Tyson.

Tyson must have run straight past, because he was gone by the time I turned human again and jumped out of the rancid vat.

Thankfully, Mum was out when I got home, so I didn't have to explain to her why I'd chosen to marinate myself in macaroni cheese and custard.

Saturday 5TH May

I just emailed Ryan to ask if he can start my training right away. I can't wait until after my exams. My lust for human meat is now so overwhelming that there's more than just embarrassment at stake. The last thing

Adventures of a Wimpy Werewolf

I want to do is freak out in my history exam and nibble the necks of everyone whose surname falls in the second half of the alphabet.

I'm pretty sure I can balance training and revision, though. I'll go round to Lunar Hall in the daytime for wolf lessons, revise in the evenings, then reward myself with twenty minutes of *Gran Turismo* before bed. Simple.

I've just got back from wolf training. Ryan's an excellent teacher, but the training was very intense. I'd planned to revise the reactivity of metals tonight, but I'm so exhausted I can hardly see my science textbook.

I turned up at Lunar Hall just after ten, and Ryan put me straight back in the manacles. This time I was happy to let him do it, as I knew I needed to be restrained for my own safety.

The first thing Ryan did was apologize. I asked him what for and he gave me the worst Chinese burn I've experienced in my life. Immediately, I felt my snout extend and my backbone wrench up.

Soon I was in full wolf form, snarling and struggling against my manacles. Once again, I was overwhelmed by my hunger for human throat. I looked at Ryan, but my instinct told me that he was a fellow wolf and wasn't on the menu. I needed to break my chains, go outside and find a proper snack.

When I was back in human form Ryan explained that for my first day of training, I'd be switching in and out of wolf mode. It was only by transforming over and over again that I'd get used to the sensation and learn how to control it.

He said that he'd have to keep annoying and upsetting me to goad me into transformation, and he didn't enjoy it any more than I did, which was weird because he looked like he was having a whale of a time.

I braced myself for another Chinese burn but he said he'd have to keep changing his methods of annoying me. Then he leant close to my face and shouted a load of anti-ginger abuse. At first it didn't bother me. I'd heard names like 'Carrot Top' and 'Ginger Biscuit' a million times before, and I found it hard to take seriously coming from a fellow ginge. But then Ryan said that I looked like Mick Hucknall from Simply Red and starting singing 'Holding Back the Years'. This brought back unpleasant memories of a boy in infant school who teased me in this exact way, and I was so upset I transformed right away.

Ryan brought on my next transformation by tickling me with a feather. He caused the one after by dangling a squeaky rubber bone in my face and pulling it away whenever I tried to bite it. And he brought on the one after that by bringing in his laptop and showing me a reality TV show called *The Only Way Is Essex*. It was so irritating it made me transform in seconds, although I must admit I found it quite absorbing once I was in wolf form.

Sunday 6TH May

I'm due back at Ryan's house at noon today, so I've woken up early for a spot of science revision. I have now looked through last year's paper and I think I'll be fine as long as exactly the same questions come up again.

Adventures of a Wimpy Werewolf

Today's training was much more civilized. Ryan taught me techniques that I can use to control my mood and prevent unwanted transformations, such as yoga, meditation, tai chi and deep breathing.

It was all proving very relaxing until I was getting up to leave and Ryan lobbed a hard rubber ball into my face. I snapped into a rage, and felt my wolf hairs coming through.

Then Ryan sat down on the floor with his legs crossed and urged me to do the same. I forced myself down, my mind torn between channelling positive energy and ripping his nose off. Eventually, I managed to calm myself down, and the hairs shrank back.

Monday 7TH May

Today was the first day of official study leave so I went straight round to Lunar Hall. When I got there, Ryan led me into his garden and fixed a steel manacle around my leg. He said that today I'd be learning how to make

myself transform. So it was up to me now. All I had
to do was picture something that would make me feel
really angry.

It was a lot harder than I expected. I tried to imagine
Tyson and think about all the times he'd called me
'Gingernut', but I felt pity rather than anger for him.
After all, he was just a silly little human who was about
to fail his exams, go out into the real world and find
out that he wasn't as important as he thought he was.
I was an alpha wolf with over a century of fun ahead.
Why should I care which biscuit he thought I resembled?

In the end I had to imagine opening my GCSE results
and finding out that I'd got an 'E' in every subject.
This had much more of an effect because I was angry
with myself for letting my revision slip. I imagined
Pete and Karl showing off their A stars while I hid
my feeble results in my pocket and I soon felt myself
transforming again.

I found that focusing on this image allowed me to
stay in wolf form, and forcing it from my mind let me
turn human again. Ryan explained that this is because
my wolf self remembers the anger associated with the
image even if it doesn't fully understand it.

All morning I went back and forth from human form to
wolf form to human form again, until inducing changes
became instinctive and natural.

Adventures of a Wimpy Werewolf

After this incredibly tough lesson, Ryan said I could move on to a more fun part of training — werewolf karate!

He dragged a sheep carcass into the garden and I had to transform and slash at it with my right paw. It was very difficult to follow instructions in wolf form. My automatic reaction was to snap at the meat with my teeth, and I couldn't understand why Ryan kept whacking me on the snout and shouting 'No!' whenever I tried. Eventually, I learned to keep my head back and lash out with my claws. When I'd managed this ten times, Ryan let me eat what was left of the sheep as a reward.

I was so tired afterwards that Ryan offered me a lift home in his Ford Fiesta. I won't be accepting his offer again, as he played his rap music too loud and drove too fast, which I found very antisocial.

Even worse, he kept shouting rude comments at other road users, which I thought was rash from someone who wants to avoid drawing attention to his species. At one point he shouted, 'Keep peddling, granddad,' at a cyclist. When the cyclist turned round, I saw it was actually Mr Landis! He looked at me and shook his head, taking it as further proof of my delinquency.

Adventures of a Wimpy Werewolf

Tuesday 8TH May

I had another good training session today. After I'd
focused on my imaginary exam results and switched into
wolf form, Ryan brought out a wheelbarrow loaded with
dead sheep. This made my wolf self howl with delight, but
Ryan said I'd have to work hard before snacking on them.

First I had to practise my clawing, then my pouncing,
then my flying kicks. Finally, he lined up all the sheep
and made me swipe their heads off one by one with my
claws. I think he said something about decapitation
being important in the upcoming battle, but I didn't
quite catch it. Finally, when I'd performed all these
moves to his satisfaction, he let me loose on the
shredded remains of the sheep.

Adventures of a Wimpy Werewolf

I felt a bit guilty when I got home because Mum had made lasagna and I wasn't remotely hungry. I could hardly tell her that I'd just eaten four entire sheep so I pretended I'd gone to Subway with my friends after school.

She somehow managed to take this as evidence that I did have a girlfriend after all, which cheered her up. She said I could hide it from her if I liked because she was no different when she started dating. Unless these first dates were to abattoirs, I suspect things were a little different, but I was happy to let her think otherwise.

Okay, I've got tonight free to revise algebra. I need to forget all about wolf stuff for the next few hours.

It's not easy, though. Tomorrow's a full moon, and the pack is gathering at Ryan's house. The pack goes to Lunar Hall for the three nights of every full moon for transformation parties.

I'm going round early to help Ryan prepare, which is very exciting. I've never helped to organize a party before. Except for my birthday trip to Pizza Hut. But that doesn't really count, as I was the only person to turn up. So technically that was a humiliating failure that I never mentioned to anyone ever again rather than a party.

Wednesday 9TH May

I've just told Mum I'm staying over at Pete's house tonight for a revision sleepover. She said she knew I was going round to see my girlfriend really, and told me not to do anything silly. I promised I wouldn't, although running around a hillside on all fours probably counts as silly in some people's books.

I know I can't really come clean about the whole wolf thing, but I still feel guilty about lying to Mum. Maybe I've just got too much of a conscience. All the more reason to avoid eating innocent humans, I suppose.

Adventures of a Wimpy Werewolf

Thursday 10TH May

It's now 7am on Thursday and I've just got home from my first—ever transformation party, which was terrific fun. I don't have much experience of parties, but I'm guessing that would count as a wild one.

I turned up at Ryan's house after lunch, and he gave me £300 in cash and sent me round all the local butchers and supermarkets to buy meat. There was loads of reduced meat in Morrisons, but I wasn't allowed to spend all the money in one place in case it drew attention to us.

Then I brought my meat back, chopped it up and laid it out in large bowls in the garden. The pack always fills up on meat as soon as they transform, which will make them much less likely to snack on any passing humans.

The first guests arrived just after eight. A few of them brought animal carcasses of their own, which was polite, and several of them made the same joke that they'd brought along a little something 'to keep the wolf from the door'.

I noticed that the other wolves were also wearing

clothes that were baggy and stretchy enough to survive transformation, like jogging bottoms, shellsuits and tracksuits, which was a relief. I was nervous enough about meeting all these new people without having to worry about seeing them starkers at the end of the night.

Ryan introduced me to everyone, and they seemed very excited to meet a new alpha wolf. I met so many people it was hard to remember their names, but I can remember a policeman called Alex, a scaffolder called Steve, a bouncer called Paul and a sixth-form student called Chloe.

I chatted to a couple from North Newchester called Alan and Janice, who said they always made sure they arrived in Lunar Hall with plenty of time to spare since the evening they got stuck in traffic on the way, transformed in their car and ruined the leather upholstery.

This led to a discussion about inconvenient transformations, which made me realize I've got off fairly lightly so far. Steve said he once got the date of the full moon mixed up and transformed at a rock festival. He was really worried he might eat loads of innocent people, but luckily none of them had showered for days, so their scent put him off.

He came round naked, covered in mud and screaming at the top of his voice at five in the morning. Luckily, this is quite normal behaviour for a rock festival so it didn't draw unwanted attention. And although the police received reports that a large wolf had been walking around on its hind legs, they also

received reports that the ghost of John Lennon had been spotted riding a unicorn, so they thought nothing of it.

The worst transformation of all, however, was Paul's first one, which happened on a transatlantic flight. Unlike Steve, he was unable to resist chomping on human flesh, and soon reduced both passengers and crew to a slurry of limbs and intestines. He got so carried away he even ate the pilot, causing the plane to crash into the sea. He was rescued by a freight ship the following day, the only survivor of a crash that claimed over fifty lives. He said it was a very harrowing introduction to world of shape—shifting, although he did at least get a decent in—flight meal for once.

By dusk, all thirty—nine members of the pack had arrived and we went out to the garden. Then we kicked off our shoes and stood in a circle, staring up at the cloudy sky and waiting for the full moon to make its first appearance.

As soon as the clouds parted, everyone in the pack began to scream at the top of their voices. The combined noise was deafening, and I made a mental note never to hold one of these parties at our house. Even if I didn't end up in prison for murder, I'd almost certainly get an ASBO for noise pollution.

One by one, the pack members dropped to all fours as their fur burst out of their skin and their snouts pushed out of their faces.

The thing that really surprised me was the huge variety of wolves they transformed into. There was a nurse called Carol who turned into a wolf with lustrous blond hair. There was a fisherman called Richard who turned into a huge muscle—bound creature that was more bear than wolf.

But perhaps the most surprising transformation was Paul. In human form, Paul was over six feet tall and had arms as thick as most people's legs. But when the moon came out, he actually shrunk in size, and ended up as a kind of werepoodle, with a pelt of curly white hair and a cute little black nose. While everyone else let out bloodcurdling howls, he yapped adorably.

When everyone had transformed, they turned to look at me expectantly. I'd been so fascinated by it all, I'd forgotten to change. I tried to make myself turn by picturing bad exam results, but it was difficult with everyone watching. It was a bit like trying to use a public toilet when other people are queuing.

I clenched my fists and tried to focus on the scene. Pete and Karl are gloating; I'm looking at my pitiful grades; even the thick kids in the school have done better than me.

Still nothing. I was more nervous than angry and I was terrified that everyone would think I was an impostor.

Noticing that I was struggling, Ryan threw a stone at me, and I used the spark of anger this inspired to transform.

After I'd changed, the other wolves barked with excitement and a couple of them came over to sniff me, which I thought was a little over-familiar. Especially when you consider where they were sniffing.

Adventures of a Wimpy Werewolf

Then it was time for dinner. After a few minutes of gnawing and chomping, the garden soon looked like a slaughterhouse after a triple shift, with blood, spittle and innards coating the grass. I usually get annoyed by messy eaters, but I didn't mind at all while I was in wolf mode.

After that, we jumped over the wall at the back of Ryan's garden and had an enjoyable dash across the moors. It felt so brilliant to run with the pack. It's not an experience I've had much in human form, as the rest of the class usually speed away from me whenever we do track events in PE. Although I did once finish in the top four in the egg and spoon race.

In wolf form, I had no problem keeping up with them all as they jumped over hedges, splashed through streams and circled frightened rabbits. Ryan even let me go up front and lead the pack a couple of times, which was fun. It must feel so brilliant to be pack leader. Maybe Ryan will let me take over if he retires one day.

As dawn broke, we changed back into human form and wandered back to Lunar Hall, nattering about where we'd been. If you'd heard us, you'd have thought

we were a rambling society rather than a pack of murderous monsters.

The only person who looked a little strange was Paul, who'd shed his jeans and t-shirt when he transformed into the werepoodle. He was now striding back in just his y-fronts, but he didn't seem too self-conscious. He's not the sort of person you'd tease about what they were wearing, even if it was just a pair of Marks & Spencer undies.

Anyway, I'm back home now and I need to rest before the party starts again tonight. Can't wait!

Mum just woke me up to ask if I was feeling all right, as I'd been in bed for the whole day. I said I'd been overdoing my revision and needed to catch up on my sleep, which seemed to convince her. One advantage of spending the first fifteen years of your life as goody two shoes is that it's easier to lie when you go off the rails.

Now I'm starting to feel guilty about getting behind with my revision. Part of me thinks I'm throwing my future away, but another part wonders why I should bother with exams at all. Maybe Ryan will let me move in with him after I finish school and help out with the pack. He might even let me be a wolf prefect. There's no harm in asking.

No, I need to push on with my revision. That way I'll have qualifications to fall back on if the whole supernatural beast thing doesn't pan out.

Friday 11TH May

I made more effort to chat to the other wolfpeople as they arrived last night. A lot of them remarked about how fast and strong I was in wolf form, which was nice.

Sadly, I don't feel that I have that much in common with the other pack members. Most of them looked at me blankly when I told them about the debating society and the chess club, and when I asked them about their hobbies, they tended to mention football. I've never really been a fan, though I haven't tried watching it in wolf form yet.

The only pack member I really connected with was the girl called Chloe. She became a werewolf when her ex-boyfriend bit her during a full moon. He then dumped her and left town, leaving her to cope with her condition alone. Luckily for her, Ryan spotted her

chasing a car a couple of months later and invited her to join the pack.

I told her about my problems balancing GCSE revision with wolf life and she said she went through the same thing last year. Her business studies exam fell on the day after a full moon, and she was still really tired from the night before, so she only got a 'D', even though she was predicted an 'A'.

This worried me, but at least us alpha wolves have a bit more flexibility. I could force myself to stay human during a full moon if I wanted to, although I'd hate to miss any of these parties.

Adventures of a Wimpy Werewolf

Shortly before midnight, we all changed again and enjoyed another night of darting across hillsides and barking at the moon. I know it doesn't sound like a whole evening's entertainment, but it feels like the most fascinating thing in the world while you're doing it.

At one point, we spotted a couple whose car had broken down on a deserted country lane. Some pack members darted ahead to eat them, and I'm ashamed to say I was one of them. But then Ryan howled angrily to us, and we returned to the pack.

Looking back, I can see that I let myself get carried away with peer pressure. It's a shame because I'm normally very good at resisting it, like that time when everyone was throwing Pete's scientific calculator around the classroom, and I caught it and returned it to him.

It certainly made me realize how lucky I was not to have been killed when I was bitten. None of the wolves I've asked so far have any memory of biting me, but whoever it was, you can bet their intention was to strip my bones like I was a KFC drumstick. I don't know what made them change their minds after one bite, but I'm incredibly glad they did.

As a reward for resisting the humans, Ryan let us attack a flock of sheep on the way back, which was very enjoyable. It's funny to think that just a few months ago, I'd been considering going vegetarian, and now I was ripping a sheep's neck open with my teeth.

It was interesting to see the different attack methods of the wolves. Alan and Janice shared a sheep between them, taking turns to hold the struggling creature down while the other enjoyed a chomp. Richard stood on his hind legs, tilted his head back, and virtually swallowed one of the poor things whole. But by far the most vicious was Paul, the yappy little werepoodle. He ripped into his sheep with amazing speed and ferocity, reducing it to a pile of bones and offal

in seconds. I made a mental note never to tease him about his wolf form.

Anyway, I'm back again now, so it's time for five hours' sleep, five hours' revision and then the third and final night of our little gathering.

Saturday 12TH May

I don't like this. I don't like this at all. I'm going to leave the pack. I'm going to tell Ryan I've had enough.

Adventures of a Wimpy Werewolf

This has all gone too far. I didn't sign up for any of this. I don't...

Sorry for the interruption to the last entry. I got so stressed I transformed while writing, which would have been very embarrassing if Mum had walked in. Luckily, I've managed to calm myself enough to return to human form now, but I'm still very stressed about what happened last night.

It all started well, with another transformation and another dash across the moors. Then when the sun came up, we all turned back into humans and hiked to Ryan's house.

Ryan said he wanted to say a few words before we went home, so we gathered in the living room.

Ryan thanked us for another enjoyable full moon, and congratulated us on resisting the stranded humans. Just when I thought he was wrapping up, he said he had a big announcement to make.

He said he'd decided that the next full moon should be the date for the vampire attack. Everyone in the pack whooped with delight when he said this, except for Chloe, who looked down at the floor.

Then Ryan pointed at me and said that now we had

another alpha wolf on our side, we were bound to defeat the vampires. This sent the pack into another frenzy of applause. He told them he'd already started my combat training and was convinced I'd be able to slice vampire heads off with a single stroke by the next full moon.

Woah, hang on a minute. Vampires? Ryan didn't mention anything about vampires when he was training me. I didn't even know they existed! You might not expect this to be a big shock to someone whose friends are nine—foot dogs, but it still takes a bit of getting used to. Who else is going to turn out to be real? Hobbits? Daleks? The Easter Bunny?

Rather than going into any more detail about the attack, Ryan then went off on a frenzied rant about how vampires were evil, and they were going to pay for what they'd done.

The whole pack let out howls of anger as Ryan spoke. I felt like I should join in, but I couldn't help wondering why we wanted to fight these creatures if they were really so merciless. Shouldn't we start by battling some less bloodthirsty creatures, like cows?

I asked Ryan if I could have a word with him when he'd finished his speech, but he told me to go home and rest before my training tomorrow.

I pointed out that my GCSEs start on Thursday and it would be more convenient for me if we could put off the attack for a while. But then Ryan said that if we were victorious, we'd own an entire island with a massive castle on it. I'd be so rich I wouldn't even bother opening my GCSE results when they came.

I agreed to go back tomorrow, but now I'm not sure. I don't want to fight any vampires. I want to focus on my exams and go to sixth form and maybe start a role-playing games club. That way I can enjoy all the excitement of battle without the danger.

Sunday 13TH May

I've only slept a couple of hours since I got back yesterday morning. Every time I drifted off to sleep I had a nightmare about battling Dracula or Nosferatu or Grandpa from *The Munsters* and got so scared I woke up in wolf form. In the end, I gave up on sleep and tried to get on with my maths revision instead. But whenever I had to add up it reminded me of The Count from *Sesame Street* and I got frightened again.

I'm not going to go round to Ryan's house today. He can fight his own vampire battle. I'm not doing it.

Adventures of a Wimpy Werewolf

Just got this email from Ryan:

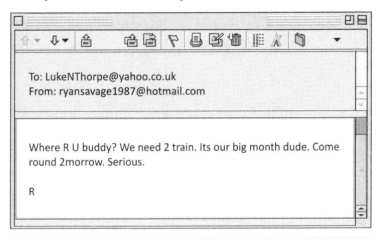

To: LukeNThorpe@yahoo.co.uk
From: ryansavage1987@hotmail.com

Where R U buddy? We need 2 train. Its our big month dude. Come round 2morrow. Serious.

R

I suppose I should at least tell him in person that I don't want to fight. I'll thank him for all his help so far, explain why I won't join his battle, come straight back here and get on with my revision. I'm sure he'll be fine with it.

Monday 14ᵀᴴ May

I'm back from Lunar Hall again now. I tried to explain to Ryan that I didn't want to fight, and he seemed to accept it. But then he said he wanted to explain a little more about vampires before I made my decision.

Ryan spoke calmly at first, but with increasing fury as he described how vampires prey on innocent humans

and leave them as drained, lifeless corpses. He said
they were feral, dirty parasites with no more right to
live than a louse or mosquito.

He asked me if I thought killing vampires was wrong
and I said that killing any living creature was wrong.
But then he said that vampires aren't actually living
creatures at all. They're just corpses brought back
to life by disease, and if you end their perverse
existences you're effectively curing them.

So even if we didn't
have a quarrel with any
particular vampires,
it was our duty to
track them down
and destroy them.
But in fact we had
been wronged by a
vampire coven, so we
had no choice but to
fight them.

Ryan said that
he'd recently
discovered
documents proving
that the remote
Scottish island of

Adventures of a Wimpy Werewolf

Hirta was stolen from the Lunar Wood Pack by a coven of vampires over a hundred years ago. The undead fiends still live in a castle on the island, and seem to think we've forgotten about their theft. Which means it's the perfect time to pay them a visit.

Next full moon, we'll all drive to Northport, and then Richard will sail us to Hirta in his trawler. Then, when the moon comes out, we'll march out onto the island and 'go and whoop some vamp'.

While we battle the vampires in wolf form, Ryan will stay human, so he can sneak around driving wooden stakes into their hearts.

After we've regained Hirta, Ryan intends to make it a safe haven for oppressed wolves, and eventually establish the largest pack in the world. Then he said as I was the only other founding alpha wolf, I'd be a natural choice for deputy leader!

I can't believe I could soon be the deputy leader of the biggest wolf pack in the world. There I was thinking I had to plough through GCSEs, A Levels and degree modules before I could get a taste of power, and I now could be in a leadership position before my sixteenth birthday.

Just imagine all the brilliant speeches I'll be able to deliver:

'Tough on vampires, tough on the causes of vampires.'

'We have nothing to fear but fear itself. And vampires.'

'We shall fight them in the graveyards, we shall fight them in the coffins...'

'Werewolves of the world unite. You have nothing to lose but your leashes.'

I was so excited about becoming the deputy leader that I let Ryan restart my training right away.

He dragged another sheep carcass out into the garden, and this time he made a cape for it out of a binbag so we could pretend it was a vampire. I transformed and worked on my claw slashes until Ryan was happy. Then I struck out at the sheep's neck and took its head off in one slice. Ryan said that if I could do that on the night, we'd defeat the fanged fiends in no time.

So I've now agreed to resume my training and fight

next full moon. I'm sure it won't effect my revision too much.

Tuesday 15TH May

I can't believe I've got my history exam tomorrow. I'm planning to revise the First World War between now and nine, the Second World War between nine and eleven, the Cold War between eleven and one, pop round to Ryan's house for some more training, and then come back and do the Russian Revolution before bed.

It's now 11pm and I've just got back from Lunar Hall. It's a bit later than I originally planned, but I think I can manage another spot of revision.

We had another good training session today. I learned the flying kick, the lightning pounce and the spinning tail attack. They were hard to get the hang of, but I know I'll be better at them by the time the full moon comes round.

I'm still frightened about facing the vampires, but the more Ryan tells me about them, the more I'm determined to destroy them. Apparently, they've been systematically stealing our land and property for centuries.

According to Ryan, us werewolves have always been in favour of peaceful coexistence, and we've drawn up countless treaties to fairly divide land. We even offered to urinate around an entire county to mark it out as our territory once. But vampires have broken their promises time and time again.

He says this is typical of their slippery evasiveness. They have hypnotic beauty and lilting, seductive voices that draw you in and trick you. This is why you have to attack them before they can speak.

By the time Ryan had finished I was ready to go up to Scotland and fight the vampires right away. I have to admit I'm feeling a little more nervous about it now I'm back home, though.

Adventures of a Wimpy Werewolf

Wednesday 16TH May

I just got back from my history exam, and I think I did a good job of keeping recent events out of my mind. At one point I got a little mixed up and wrote that the Nazis were 'as bad as the vampires', but I'm sure the examiners will dismiss this as a figure of speech. I don't think I'll get an A star, but I'm sure I passed. Under the circumstances, that's not bad going.

Adventures of a Wimpy Werewolf

I'd originally planned to take the afternoon off, but I started thinking about vampires and it made me so angry I went right round to Lunar Hall to continue my training. Ryan said he was impressed by my dedication to the cause, and repeated his promise to make me deputy leader.

After practising neck slashes for an hour, I asked Ryan if the vampires wouldn't just turn into bats and fly away when we tried to attack them.

He laughed and said that was just a silly myth, which I thought was a bit rich coming from someone who spends much of his time as a large pack animal.

Apparently, loads of the stuff you hear about vampires isn't true. They can't be killed by sunlight, but they can be killed if you ram a wooden stake into their hearts or remove their heads.

It's true that they hate garlic and crucifixes, but it's not true that they sleep in coffins filled with soil, as they don't sleep at all. I wish I didn't have to sleep. I could fit training and revision in really easily if it wasn't for boring old sleep.

They can be seen in mirrors and photographs, although they try to avoid the latter because they would prove that they don't age, and this would bring them to the attention of their legions of human fans.

The more I find out about vampires, the less I

understand why humans love them so much. They're blood—guzzling corpses. How exactly is that sexy? It's outrageous that we should allow teenage girls to put posters of them on their walls. We wouldn't let them do it with any other mass murderers.

Thursday 17TH May

This is all very confusing. I was about to plough through my science revision this morning when Mum burst into my room with a massive grin on her face. She said my girlfriend was here, and I looked out the window and saw that Chloe from the pack was standing at the door.

I dashed downstairs, popping a Smint into my mouth just in case she actually had come round for a date. When I got to the door, Chloe said we should go to the park where no one could overhear us, which I'm ashamed to say raised my hopes further.

Unfortunately, romance wasn't on her mind. Instead, she asked me what I thought about Ryan's plan to attack the vampires. I repeated everything he'd told me about how the island was stolen from our pack and how aggressive vampires were. But then Chloe asked if we weren't the ones who were acting aggressively. Also, if we had Lunar Hall and they had their island, why couldn't we just leave each other to live in peace?

Chloe said she'd tried to discourage Ryan when he'd told her about his plan three months ago, but he wouldn't be swayed. Now the attack was approaching, all she could do was visit everyone in the pack individually and convince them that war was wrong. She invited me to come along and I told her I'd consider it.

The more I think about it, the more I think Chloe might be right. I'm sure vampires are just as evil as Ryan claims, but that doesn't mean we should invade their island. Wasps are pretty horrible too, but I don't feel the urge to pick up one of their nests and smash it on the floor.

I've always been a pacifist, and I don't see why that should change now. Admittedly, I spend a lot more time wanting to sink my teeth into the throats of innocents as if they were raspberry doughnuts, but that's no reason why I shouldn't seek peaceful solutions to problems when I'm in human form.

I'll email Ryan and tell him I need a break from training to focus on my exams. Then I'll go around with Chloe and convince the rest of the pack to boycott the war. When enough of them have signed up, we can all tell Ryan at the same time, and he'll have to accept it. After all, he can hardly battle the vampires alone.

Mum just came into my room and asked me loads of questions about Chloe. I kept insisting she wasn't my girlfriend, but she was having none of it. In the end, I pretended she was so I could get on

with my revision. But that only made Mum go on about
how I should treat my girlfriend with respect and not
like how Dad treated her. I closed my textbook and put
my pens away. I knew from experience that when *that*
conversation starts, I could pretty much write off the
rest of the evening.

Friday 18TH May

Chloe called round again just before lunch, and was
overjoyed when I agreed to join her peace campaign. She
said that with the backing of an alpha werewolf, it
would be much easier to win the other wolves over.

Then she showed me a map with the addresses of all
the pack members marked on. They're scattered within
a forty—mile radius of Lunar Hall, so this is going to
take a while, but we thought we might as well make a
start on the nearest ones.

The first member we visited was the scaffolder called
Steve. He looks like he's in his mid—twenties, but it's
quite hard to tell with wolves. He could be fifty for all
I know. He wasn't in when we called round so we followed
his scent to a nearby construction site.

Adventures of a Wimpy Werewolf

He was happy to come and speak to us, but he couldn't believe we were being serious when we said we wanted to prevent the battle. He kept slapping me on the back and telling me what a classic windup it was. Then he said he had to get back to work, but he was looking forward to seeing me at the rumble with the vampires.

The next member we tried was Paul, the bouncer who turns into the werepoodle. He was very friendly at first, and invited us inside his terraced house for tea and giblets. But when we tried to recruit him for our peace campaign, he got really angry and threw us out. He said that vampires were the most evil creatures on earth and he'd been waiting his entire life for a chance to have a pop at them.

Chloe asked him if he'd ever met a vampire, and he seemed to find the very question offensive, saying that if he'd even been within sniffing distance of one, he'd have ripped its head off and turned it into an ashtray. He then suggested that we leave before he did the same to us.

The only other pack members in walking distance were Alan and Janice, who lived in a semi-detached house in the northern suburbs of Newchester. By the time we found their house, it was early evening, and they were watching a *Shaun the Sheep* DVD with their five-year-old son. I wonder if they were explaining that those are the animals that mummy and daddy ate alive last full moon.

They wouldn't let us in, but we were allowed to whisper to them in the porch. It was hard to put our point across this way, and we didn't get very far. They said they were sure Ryan had the best interests of the pack at heart and they were happy to go along with whatever he wanted. Then they said they had to go before their son asked who we were.

You can't blame them, really. With two werewolf parents, that boy's almost certain to turn wolf as soon as he hits puberty, so they just want to give him as normal a life as possible until then. But he's going to find it a lot harder to adjust to the change if he loses both his parents in a supernatural battle. Imagine if he ends up in an orphanage. It will be like putting a furry time bomb in there.

It's going to be harder than we thought to convince the pack not to fight. I've agreed to meet up with Chloe again tomorrow so we can rethink our approach. In the meantime, I've got my science exam on Monday so it's fossil fuels time for me.

Saturday 19TH May

Chloe came round this afternoon and I showed her up to my bedroom. Mum kept coming in to ask if we wanted anything and she was really staring at Chloe. I could tell she wanted me to introduce her, but we had more important things to get on with so I ignored her.

Adventures of a Wimpy Werewolf

As a result of our brainstorm, Chloe and I have decided to form the Werewolf Peace Front. I think the other wolves will find it easier to get behind our cause if we make it a proper organization with leaflets and stickers.

We've already designed a logo of a werewolf's paw making a peace sign, and devised slogans like 'Keep the wolf from the war' and 'I'm a sheep in wolves' clothing'.

I'm not saying the other wolves are stupid, but I think they'll find these kinds of soundbites easier to follow than complex arguments.

We've also come up with the following ideas to promote our cause:

* Hold a peace protest outside Ryan's house (Chloe's idea)

This was vetoed by me on the grounds that I'm still incredibly frightened of him.

* Devise an anti-war piece of drama (my idea)

This was rejected by Chloe on the grounds that

theatre is not a medium appreciated by the other wolves, as she found when she tried to organize a pack trip to Stratford-upon-Avon last year.

* Stay in bed together for a week to promote peace like John Lennon and Yoko Ono (my idea)
   This was rejected by Chloe.

* Produce anti-war badges (my idea)
   This was approved, as I still have the badge-making machine I used for the chess club and the debating society.

* celebrity endorsement (my idea)
   This was initially rejected as too difficult to organize, but then we realized we could just use the celebrities without asking them. My first suggestions for campaign spokesmen were Stephen Fry and Sir Ian McKellen, but after consulting with Chloe about the cultural interests of the pack, we have now produced a leaflet that reads: 'Wayne Rooney says, "No to war with vampires."'

*Write a protest song (Chloe's idea)

This was approved, as Chloe's dad owns an acoustic guitar.

Chloe has now gone home to write her song and I've produced forty badges with the slogan 'War with vampires? No fangs.' That should be enough to avert supernatural apocalypse for now. In the meantime, back to the science revision!

Sunday 20TH May

I had a good revision session this morning, then Chloe came round and played her protest song. At first I thought she was tuning the guitar and warming up her voice, but after a while I realized it was the actual song.

The song's called 'Fangs and Fur' and the only lyrics in it are, 'Fangs and fur, peace not war'. I wouldn't

say it was a pleasant experience, but protest songs aren't necessarily meant to be. So what if Chloe sounds like a dog with its tail trapped in a car door when she sings? I once saw a clip of a very famous protest singer called Bob Dylan, and if anything his voice was even worse.

I pretended to like the song and then we set out to visit the next wolves on our map. The first we visited was Dave, who works as a shopfitter in South Newchester. I could tell he was going to be a tough sell, but we did our best to explain our cause anyway. He seemed interested in the Wayne Rooney leaflet, but I could tell the finer points of our argument weren't sinking in. After a few minutes he stopped us to say that he wasn't interested in politics. Then Chloe launched into her protest song, and he slammed the door in our faces.

From there we took a bus to a small village south of Newchester called High Oak where a pack member called Sarah lives in a detached house called 'The Hollyhocks'. She seemed to have a much more open mind, and happily accepted the badges and leaflets we offered. She even sat politely through Chloe's song, although she winced slightly during the tenth chorus.

In the end, she said we'd won her over and agreed to boycott the battle, which was a bit of a result. Even if we only convince half the pack to do the same, it will make Ryan rethink his plans. It just goes to show the power of peaceful protest.

Anyway, no more time for this. I've got my science exam tomorrow.

Monday 21ST May

I don't think that went too badly. I wouldn't say I got everything right, but I certainly did better than on that test when my hands turned into paws. I got a bit stuck on the section about the human body, because it made me wonder about the biology of werewolves.

Adventures of a Wimpy Werewolf

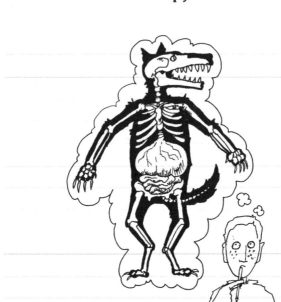

Nothing I've been taught so far can explain why I have the power to change my muscles and bones, so why should I bother with science at all? What else don't they know?

Despite my disillusionment with the limits of human knowledge, I managed to answer most of the questions, so I'm pretty sure I didn't fail.

Whatever Ryan's motives were, I'm still grateful he trained me to control my transformations. I couldn't have done my exams at all if he hadn't. The invigilators are so strict they don't let anyone out of the hall. I bet even a species change wouldn't count as a good enough excuse.

Adventures of a Wimpy Werewolf

Just got this email from Ryan:

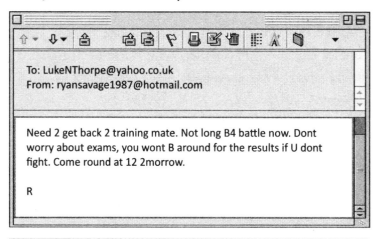

To: LukeNThorpe@yahoo.co.uk
From: ryansavage1987@hotmail.com

Need 2 get back 2 training mate. Not long B4 battle now. Dont worry about exams, you wont B around for the results if U dont fight. Come round at 12 2morrow.

R

I can't work out if he means I won't be around because the vampires will kill me, or if he's threatening me personally.

I suppose I could keep my training up until we've convinced enough wolves to revolt against him. My next exam isn't until Thursday, so I can probably fit it in.

Tuesday 22ND May

Ryan was very friendly when I turned up, which should have made me suspicious, given that I'd missed three days of training. We went out into the garden, transformed and practised attack moves. I really

Adventures of a Wimpy Werewolf

enjoyed the exercise while I was in my wolf state, and I forgot all about the peace movement.

After this, Ryan fixed manacles around my legs and said we had to start another vital phase of training. I should have turned human again and questioned what he was doing, but you're very trusting of your pack leader when you're in wolf form.

Then Ryan picked up a stick, threw it to the other end of the garden and shouted 'Fetch!' I instinctively ran after it, and the manacles on my legs made me fall flat on my face. He repeated this over and over again, sniggering to himself.

Next Ryan brought out a Hello Kitty soft toy and fixed it to my tail with a rubber band. I kept spotting the annoying cat out of the corner of my eye and trying to rip it to shreds. But every time I pounced, it leapt out of the way just as fast. Obviously, I can see what the problem was now, but it wasn't easy to understand as a wolf. I just kept spinning round and round and tripping over my manacles, and still the hateful white cat wagged in and out of my field of vision.

Finally, Ryan stuck a paper bag over my head. To my confused wolf brain, it seemed that I was trapped in a tiny room with no doors and windows and I began to howl with terror. Eventually I managed to calm down enough to turn human again, and the bag and toy fell away.

I asked Ryan what the point of this training was, and he said it wasn't training at all. It was punishment. Then he showed me an envelope Sarah had sent him containing our anti-war leaflet and badge, and a full outline of what we'd said to her.

I can't believe she grassed us up! I know I reported my fair share of pupils for smoking and fighting when I was a prefect, but there was no excuse for sneakiness this time. All we wanted to do was prevent violent conflict.

Ryan asked me to explain myself, so I thought I might as well tell the truth. I said that I didn't see why we couldn't just leave the vampires to their island. After all, we still had Lunar Hall, so why couldn't we be satisfied with that?

This sent him off on another massive rant about how untrustworthy vampires are. He said they could turn up and attack us at any time of the day or night, and we weren't safe until we wiped them out.

Adventures of a Wimpy Werewolf

Then he said he'd have to go away and decide what to do, leaving me to strain uselessly against my manacles.

Ryan came back a couple of hours later and said he'd let me go free if I agreed to fight. He said he'd spoken to Chloe, and she'd confessed to being the ringleader of the conspiracy. He'd formally excluded her from the pack, and I had to promise never to speak to her again.

He said that I deserved another chance, as it would be very useful for him to have another alpha werewolf in the attack. However, if I showed any more signs of disloyalty, he would personally rip my throat out.

Adventures of a Wimpy Werewolf

Now I'm back home and trying to revise for my English exam. I'm so tired I can barely lift up my pen, but I have to try.

I don't want Ryan to rip my throat out. I'll never win another debating society trophy with no throat.

Wednesday 23RD May

Today I'm going to have a normal day. I'm not going to do anything weird and I'm not going to speak to any shape-shifters. I'm just going to get on with my revision and forget all about wolves and vampires.

Chloe keeps leaving messages on my phone, while Ryan keeps sending emails to check I'm still on his side, but I'm ignoring them all.

Thursday 24TH May

Thanks to my full day of revision, I think my English exam went pretty well. Luckily for me, one of the options was to write an essay arguing either for or against the war in Afghanistan. I chose the anti-war stance, and wrote a very passionate essay that helped me let off steam about my recent problems.

To be honest, I think I kept getting the two conflicts muddled in my mind, like when I said that Americans only fight during full moons and the Taliban are allergic to garlic. But they mark you on the clarity of your argument rather than factual accuracy, so it should be fine.

When I got out of the exam hall, Chloe was waiting for me at the school gates. I wanted to ignore her, but everyone kept asking if she was my girlfriend, so I thought I might as well pretend she was to boost my street cred.

I told her that Ryan had threatened to rip my throat out if I had anything else to do with the peace movement, and she said that warmongering despots always use violence to get their own way.

I asked her if there was anything we could do to prevent the attack, and she said she had a plan but she wanted to tell me about it before going ahead with it.

Then she told me something so depraved and horrible it made me wish I'd never spoken to her in the first place.

Chloe has met and spoken with actual vampires! Worse than that, she had a vampire boyfriend once! He was called Nigel, and he went to the same school as her. And at the start of last year, he moved up to Scotland to live in the very coven that Ryan wants to attack next full moon. So that's why she was so concerned about the battle!

Now Chloe wants to tip off Nigel about the upcoming attack so he can help us resolve the conflict peacefully. I told her I wanted no part in negotiations with undead fiends and that if she didn't abandon her plan right away, I'd tell Ryan.

Then she tried to convince me that vampires aren't as bad as Ryan makes out, but I didn't listen to her lies. She even had the cheek to claim that I reminded her of the one called Nigel! I was so incensed that I told her never to contact me again.

143

Adventures of a Wimpy Werewolf

Friday 25TH May

It all seems so obvious now. Chloe has consorted with vampires, and their seductive words have wormed their way into her brain and blinded her from the truth. It's just like Ryan said. Give them a few seconds and their lilting voices and mesmeric beauty will hypnotize you into believing their dangerous falsehoods.

I thought Chloe was an honest pacifist, but it turns out she was an agent for the forces of darkness all along. They nearly infected me too, poisoning my brain with their depraved trickery.

Anyway, the good news is that they didn't, so I'm free to get on with my geography homework. I'm doing tectonic plates tonight, which should hopefully take my mind off evil beings for a while.

Adventures of a Wimpy Werewolf

Saturday 26ᵀᴴ May

Chloe turned up at our house again this lunchtime, and Mum showed her in. Mum was really grinning again, as if she knew what was going on. She wouldn't be grinning if she really did know what was going on. She'd be grabbing a crucifix and sobbing with terror. Still, there's no point trying to explain any of it to her. She wouldn't understand.

I pretended to be pleased to see Chloe, but when Mum had gone, I had a go at her for coming round when I said I didn't want to talk to her. She said that she just wanted another chance to convince me that vampires weren't as bad as I'd heard. I said her mind had been corrupted by their lies and she'd become a vessel for their evil.

She then produced a scrap of paper containing a poem that the vampire called Nigel had written for her before he went to Scotland. She began to read it, so I shoved my fingers in my ears, determined to protect myself from the seductive words. But as the poem went on, it didn't seem very dangerous or alluring at all. It just seemed a bit... well.. rubbish.

'Though You May Be Far Away'
By Nigel Mullet, aged 100

Though you may be far away
You'll still be in my heart,
For we are joined together
Although we're far apart.

We may never meet again
In this world or the next,
But if you want to get in touch
You could always text.

When Chloe finished the poem, I waited to see if the words brainwashed me into lusting after the shadowy realm of the undead, but nothing happened.

Then she showed me some passport photos she'd taken with Nigel in the train station booth. Let's just say that if vampires really do have an alluring supernatural beauty, it doesn't come across in photographs. Maybe if she'd had a picture of a female vampire it would have been easier for me to judge.

The more she described Nigel, the more it seemed that he wasn't very scary at all. He even joined a chess club once, although he prefers computer games.

After a while I agreed that if Nigel was really as normal as she claimed, we might as well ask for his advice. I still didn't fancy taking part in a supernatural battle, despite everything I'd promised Ryan.

Adventures of a Wimpy Werewolf

Sunday 27TH May

Chloe got back in touch with Nigel today, and I have to say I'm feeling much more relaxed about the whole thing now.

From: Chloesparrow@live.com
To: nigelmullet@hotmail.com
Cc: LukeNThorpe@yahoo.co.uk

Hey Fangy

Sorry to contact you out of the blue, but got a bit of a prob with the local wolves and wondered if you could help.
 FYI I am copying in my friend Luke. Hope you don't mind.
 Hope you and family are enjoying the new coven. Not too cold I hope!

Love Chloe

From: nigelmullet@hotmail.com
To: Chloesparrow@live.com
Cc: LukeNThorpe@yahoo.co.uk

Chloe!!! Long time no see!!!

Things are great here, loving the coven. I don't really feel temperature but I expect it's very cold. Our blood supplies froze last winter so we all had to have blood lollipops for a whole week. They were lovely, though.

Family are fine. Sadly, my sister has joined the vampire Glee club, so we'll have to sit through another one of her concerts soon. I wish I could say she'll grow out of it, but obviously we'll all be the same age for ever!

Any problems with the fleabags just fire away. Who is this Luke guy?

Best

Nige
V^^^^V

Adventures of a Wimpy Werewolf

From: Chloesparrow@live.com
To: nigelmullet@hotmail.com
Cc: LukeNThorpe@yahoo.co.uk

Luke is another wolf, but you can trust him.

The problem is a bit of a biggie, I'm afraid.

Earlier this year I joined a wolf pack based in Lunar Hall, to the north of Newchester. The leader of this pack, Ryan Savage, believes that your island of Hirta was originally a wolf settlement. He has recently found documents that prove it belongs to our pack, and he intends to retake the island by force during the next full moon. Awkward!!!

Luke and I have tried campaigning for peace, but everyone is determined to go ahead. What do you suggest we do?

Sorry to drop it on you like this.

Chloe

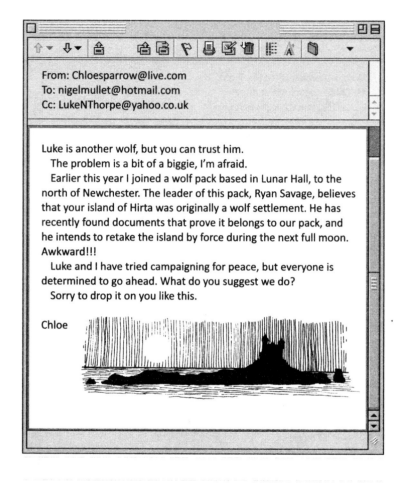

Adventures of a Wimpy Werewolf

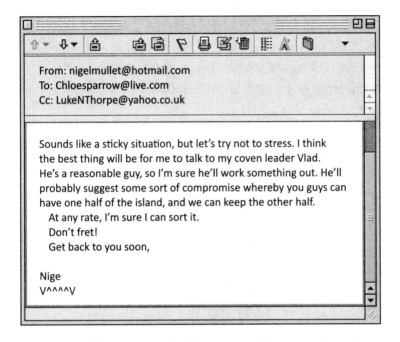

From: nigelmullet@hotmail.com
To: Chloesparrow@live.com
Cc: LukeNThorpe@yahoo.co.uk

Sounds like a sticky situation, but let's try not to stress. I think the best thing will be for me to talk to my coven leader Vlad. He's a reasonable guy, so I'm sure he'll work something out. He'll probably suggest some sort of compromise whereby you guys can have one half of the island, and we can keep the other half.

At any rate, I'm sure I can sort it.
Don't fret!
Get back to you soon,

Nige
V^^^^V

Nigel seems to have everything under control, so hopefully we can get all this sorted out soon. That's quite a weight off my mind. Back to the geography revision for me.

Monday 28TH May

I think I did pretty well on my geography exam this afternoon. I won't go as far as to predict that I'll get an A star, but I reckon I'll get at least a B when they take my coursework into account.

Adventures of a Wimpy Werewolf

After the exam, Pete asked if the girl who'd come to meet me on Thursday was my girlfriend, so I pretended she was. He asked me how I managed to get an older girlfriend, so I said I got off with her in a nightclub, but it wasn't a big deal.

He then tried to boast about how he'd completed the latest *Uncharted* game on difficult mode, but I just shrugged. Older girlfriend beats gaming skill and he knew it. I know she isn't actually my girlfriend, but it's only fair that my condition should win me some sort of cool points after all the embarrassment it's caused.

Unfortunately, I hung around for so long that Tyson spotted me and announced that we were having a fight. I've had so much on my plate recently that I'd completely forgotten about the day I clawed him on the back of the head.

Before long, word about the fight spread around the playground and a massive crowd gathered round us to watch.

Tyson shoved me a few times, and then waited for a reaction. At first I was terrified I'd transform, but I managed to stay calm and stay human.

I wasn't entirely sure what I could do. I couldn't turn into a wolf with everyone watching, but on the other hand, I couldn't run away and let this pathetic little human beat me.

Instead, I leapt up into the air and attempted a flying kick. If I'd performed this move in wolf form I'd have split Tyson in two, but the human version wasn't exactly lethal. I managed to brush his chest with my foot, but I landed awkwardly and hurt myself more than him.

It worked, though. Tyson was so shocked he turned and ran out of the school gates in tears, to a clamour of shame coughs. Someone in the crowd shouted 'Luke's a ginger ninja!' and everyone laughed. I'm glad I'm leaving school, as this would almost certainly have become my

Adventures of a Wimpy Werewolf

nickname. Still, it's better than 'Copper Top' or 'Ginger Minger', isn't it?

Tuesday 29TH May

I woke up this morning to see that Tyson had posted back my copy of *Grand Theft Auto*. He hadn't included a note of apology, but it was a definite sign of submission.

So I was feeling pretty good as I settled down for a celebratory game. The war was off, I was getting back on top of my work and everyone at school thought I was the Karate Kid. I must remind myself never to tempt fate by thinking so positively ever again.

When I turned on my computer, I saw the following email:

From: nigelmullet@hotmail.com
To: Chloesparrow@live.com
Cc: LukeNThorpe@yahoo.co.uk

Sorry guys, bit of a spanner in the works regarding the wolf thing. I talked to Vlad and he said that vampires have been living on this island for the past thousand years and any attempt to claim otherwise was 'typical of the dishonesty of those mangy curs'. Sorry about the wolfist language, but I'm quoting directly.

I told him about the plan to attack and he said the 'full force of the vampire army will be waiting for those scabby mongrels' and he'll make it his personal responsibility to make sure that no wolf leaves this island with its head still on its shoulders.

He then called a coven meeting and announced that we were instigating an official battle with the Lunar Wood Pack under international supernatural law. He's now signed a proclamation of battle and sent it to the head of your pack and alerted both the Vampire Council and the Werewolf Council.

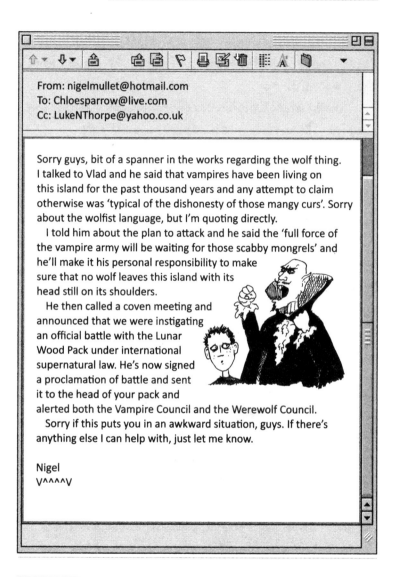

Sorry if this puts you in an awkward situation, guys. If there's anything else I can help with, just let me know.

Nigel
V^^^^V

Adventures of a Wimpy Werewolf

An awkward situation? We've just stoked up the most deadly conflict in the history of earth. It's a bit more than awkward.

I thought Nigel said his coven leader was a reasonable vampire. I'd hate to meet an unreasonable one!

It looks like Ryan was right about vampires all along. They're warlike and deadly. Just because Chloe met one who was a bit pathetic, she started to believe they were rational beings.

She was wrong, and now we're just over a week away from a deadly conflict. It couldn't have happened at a worse time, either. I've got my French exam on Friday and that's my worst subject.

Wednesday 30TH May

Chloe just called round at my house again. She looked really stressed, and kept looking out the window to see if Ryan was coming. I told her that he probably hadn't even received the battle proclamation yet, and even if he had he might spare her life, or at least kill her fairly painlessly.

I don't think this helped, because she said she had to leave town right away so he couldn't find her. She said she was going to head north and find a bed and breakfast while she worked out what to do.

Adventures of a Wimpy Werewolf

I think she was expecting me to come along, but I really need to get on with my French revision. If I felt like I'd aced my oral and listening tests earlier in the year it would be a different story, but I've got a lot riding on the final exam.

I know there are lots of exciting things happening at the moment, but it doesn't mean that knowledge is no longer important. For example, what if I have to battle some evil French vampires one day? Then I'll be glad I can understand them. As long as they don't use any adjectives. I haven't had time to revise those.

Mais, où est le sang?

Zut alors!

Adventures of a Wimpy Werewolf

I told Chloe to call me once she'd worked out what we should do and she ran off to the station.

Thursday 31ST May

Ryan just called round at our house! I can't believe he came here! Mum was really concerned when she saw him, and asked if he was Chloe's ex-boyfriend. I told her he was a school friend who'd come round to help me revise French, but she wasn't convinced.

Ryan came up to my bedroom and searched in the wardrobe and under the bed for Chloe. I told him I didn't know where she was, but he insisted that her scent was all over the room. Then I admitted that she'd called round, but pretended I'd refused to speak to her because of her disloyalty to the pack.

He looked like he was about to attack, but then he slapped me on my shoulder and said he knew I was one of the good ones.

Then he showed me the ancient scroll Vlad had sent him:

Dear Ryan

You are hereby formally invited to battle the Hirta Coven at the full moon beginning June 8th. The battle will be fought in accordance with international supernatural law. Failure to observe this notice will result in us hunting you down like the putrid strays you are.

Yours sincerely

Vladamir Carpathian
Hirta Castle
Hirta

I pretended to be shocked by Vlad's announcement and said it had made me more determined than ever to slash some vampire heads off.

Ryan said he knew Chloe was responsible, and he intended to tear her limbs off and stuff them down her throat in front of the rest of us to show what happens to traitors. I told him this was better than she deserved.

Then Ryan got down on his hands and knees

Adventures of a Wimpy Werewolf

and followed Chloe's scent out of our house. He won't get further than the train station, but at least it got rid of him.

I asked Mum to help with my French revision so she wouldn't see Ryan crawling away down the street. She said that I shouldn't worry about it because when she went to Calais on a booze cruise, most of them spoke English anyway. Great, so I'll just write that on my exam paper, shall I?

Friday 1ST June

Okay, well that could have been worse. My French exam, I mean. Not the situation between the vampires and werewolves. That couldn't really be worse. But I've got over a week until my maths exam, which should be ample time to get all this nonsense sorted out.

I've just called Chloe, and she's staying in a cheap bed and breakfast in the seaside town of Southpool. I'm going up there on Monday so we can work out how to stop the battle.

In the meantime I'm going to train with Ryan again, so he doesn't suspect I'm still part of the resistance.

Chloe mentioned that Nigel's also going to do his best to help. I'm not sure I want him to. If last time is anything to go by, his help will probably result in an army of flesh-eating ogres joining the battle on the side of the vampires.

Saturday 2ND June

I've just got back from Lunar Hall. Ryan's going mental with all this war stuff now. Sometimes when he talks about vampires, he gets so angry that he turns into a wolf and doesn't even realize he's barking instead of speaking, which is hardly a sign that he's dealing with things rationally.

I asked Ryan how his plans had changed now we're fighting an official battle that's registered with the vampire and werewolf councils. He said it means we have to observe supernatural law, which forbids the use of wooden stakes and silver bullets. The battle will last for the three nights of the next full moon, and if neither side is victorious during that time, it will continue a month later.

I asked him what would happen if he used wooden stakes and he said that full war would be declared, and every werewolf pack and vampire coven in the world would be obliged to join in.

Then a strange look came into his eyes and he asked if it would be such a bad thing if the war did start again. After all, why should we rid the world of just one vampire coven when we could rid it of the whole lot?

Then he confessed his true plans. He's going to fight the first two nights in accordance with the law. But if we haven't won by the third night, he's going to fetch his secret stash of wooden stakes from Richard's boat and finish off as many vampires as he can. He even claimed that as a fellow alpha, it was my duty to join in with this shocking act of vampicide.

I tried to convince him to fight an honest and legal battle, but he was having none of it. He asked me to consider immortality for a moment. He said that at first it would be a blast. You could cross the road without looking, insult hard people and ignore the safety demonstrations on planes. But after a couple of centuries, the weariness would set in and you'd be craving oblivion.

He said that even though vampires might not admit it to themselves, the truth is they all want to die. That's why they spend so long moping around in graveyards and listening to funeral dirges. He'll be doing them a favour when he brings out the stakes. They'll probably be flinging themselves on them and thanking him for ending their obscene existences.

I pretended that he'd convinced me, and vowed to continue my training at home. He's getting so obsessed with his hatred for vampires that I doubt he'll notice when I don't come back.

Adventures of a Wimpy Werewolf

Sunday 3ᴿᴰ June

I'm all packed and ready to set off for Southpool first thing tomorrow, but there's something I need to do before I leave. The guilt of lying to Mum has finally caught up with me. I'm going to tell her the truth and I'm going to do it now. What if I end up getting killed by a vampire? She'll never know what happened to me. This is the least I owe her.

Well, that didn't work. I went into the living room and announced to Mum that I wanted to tell her about my true nature. Without waiting for another word, she hugged me and said she couldn't be happier that I was gay. She said she couldn't wait for us to go clothes shopping together and have a good old natter about men.

I told her that she'd got the wrong end of the stick entirely, so she asked what I wanted to tell her.

I tried to force out the words, 'Mum, I'm a werewolf,' but I just couldn't. She's been through so much since Dad left that I couldn't bring myself to tell her that her only child is a throat-chomping monstrosity.

Instead, I told her that Chloe and I were in love and that we'd decided to go youth hostelling in Scotland

together. She said she was very happy
for me, and gave me twenty quid. I
said I'd do my best
to call her when I
had reception.

After that I went
to the cashpoint
and took out all my
birthday money, so overall
I should have enough for the next week or so. I was going
to save up for a new laptop, but I suppose I won't need
one if a full supernatural war kicks off and the world is
plunged into medieval chaos, so this takes priority.

Monday 4TH June

I arrived in Southpool a couple of hours ago and Chloe
was very pleased to see me. I suggested that we should
share a room to save money, but she wasn't keen on the
idea, so I've booked into a single room.

It wasn't very expensive anyway. It's surprising how
empty this town is in the height of summer. There must
be no one at all here for the rest of the year.

Adventures of a Wimpy Werewolf

Not that there's very much to do. There are a couple of cafes, a couple of amusement arcades and a derelict fairground but that's about it. The beach is nice, though the sea's very brown.

Chloe just told me that Nigel has agreed to join our anti-war group. Apparently, he's sailing here tomorrow in his dad's fishing boat to help us plan our resistance activities.

I can't believe I'm going to meet an actual vampire! I wonder if I'll be freaked out. I've met so many werewolves now that you'd think I'd be used to the whole mythical creatures thing. But the idea of vampires, with their fangs and capes and pale skin, still gives me the collywobbles. I hope he doesn't try and drink my blood. I've always hated injections, and I bet vampire bites are ten times worse.

We're putting off the next meeting of the peace front until Nigel gets here, so I suppose this would be a good chance for some maths revision. I might draw up an agenda for tomorrow's meeting first, though. You can't be too prepared at times like this.

Tuesday 5TH June

Nigel arrived in Southpool just after lunch. He paid for a room in the bed and breakfast, even though he doesn't really need one because he doesn't sleep. He just thought it would help us look more like a casual group of school friends and less like a bunch of *Scooby Doo* villains.

I wasn't freaked out at all when I finally met him. You'd never guess he was dead if you saw him walking down the street. He was wearing jeans and a t-shirt rather than a cape and he seemed to have normal teeth rather than fangs. He had pale skin, and his hand was really cold when I shook it, but he looked less like a vampire than most goths. Ryan had warned me that vampires smell of evil and decay when you meet them, but Nigel just smelled of Lynx Africa. (24)

I waited for him to speak in case his voice was seductive and mesmerizing, but our conversation was more awkward than hypnotic. I asked him if he'd had a good journey, and he said the sea had been fairly calm. Then he asked me about my train journey and I told him I'd missed my connection at Westchester and had to wait in Costa Coffee, but I didn't mind

because I got a sofa. As far as conversations between werewolves and vampires go, it probably wasn't up there with the classics.

After that I broke the news to them about Ryan's scheme to use wooden stakes on the third night of the battle. I think Nigel might have gone even paler than usual when I revealed this, though I can't be sure. He then disclosed that Vlad was planning to use silver bullets on the final night of the battle. Nigel had pointed out that this would lead to full supernatural war, but Vlad had said he'd welcome a chance to prove vampire superiority once and for all.

It sounds like Ryan and Vlad deserve each other. I wish we could just arrange an arm wrestle between them so they could leave the rest of us to live in peace. But it's all gone too far now. They've stoked up their armies, a battle is coming, ancient laws will be broken and the most deadly conflict of all will return, unless we act.

With this in mind, we moved onto the first point on my agenda, which was the renaming of the Werewolf Peace Front to reflect its new diversity. I liked 'The Werewolf and Vampire Peace Front' while Nigel preferred the 'The Vampire and Werewolf Anti-War Movement'. In the end Chloe insisted we call ourselves 'The Alliance of Peaceful Supernaturals' and have done with it.

Adventures of a Wimpy Werewolf

Looking back, this wasn't a great use of our time, but it seemed incredibly important. Whenever I see politicians arguing on the TV, I get angry that they can't put their differences aside and actually do something about the problems of the world, but now I see how easy it is to be distracted by trivial discussions.

Even after we'd agreed that the movement's new logo should be a werewolf and vampire shaking hands, it took us over an hour to agree which hand should appear on the left.

At one point in our discussion, I saw that Nigel's teeth extend into fangs. He took a flask out of his bag and sipped from it, and they shrunk right back up again. I tried not to stare, but I couldn't look away, like that time I saw a woman breastfeeding on the train.

I suppose Nigel must have human blood in his flask, which is pretty horrible. I know I eat live animals and everything, but sipping cold blood must be absolutely minging. I don't even like tasting my own blood if I get a nosebleed.

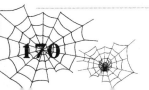

Wednesday 6TH June

The Alliance of Peaceful Supernaturals reconvened early this morning to move on to the third point on my agenda, which was the election of president and treasurer. Chloe pointed out that we should probably jump ahead to point twenty—seven, preventing the battle, as the full moon was only two days away.

We both agreed and I got the ball rolling with the suggestion that we hide here in Southpool until the whole thing's blown over. Nigel was very open to this, but Chloe said it was out of the question. If we allow the battle to go ahead, it could lead to a devastating war that could see the extinction of the vampire, werewolf and human races. Fine, I was just blue—sky thinking. It was supposed to be brainstorm, after all.

Next, Chloe suggested that we form a third army and declare war on both sides, forcing them to bond together to kill us. Nigel and I weren't keen on this idea as it involved our brutal murder.

Then Nigel suggested we write down a list of our skills and think about how we could apply them to the problem, which I thought very sensible.

171

Adventures of a Wimpy Werewolf

Luke

Speed
Strength
Chess
Debating
Computer Games

Chloe

Speed
Strength
Acoustic Guitar
Singing
Designing Placards

Nigel

Speed
Strength
Poetry
Piano
Computer Games

We had to discount strength and speed, as all vampires and werewolves have these, so they aren't really an advantage. But I think we came up with a good plan using our other skills.

We'll sail up to Hirta on Friday, and wait for both armies to gather. Then, just as they're about to clash, we'll run out into the middle of the battlefield carrying placards and loudhailers. Nigel will read out a poem about peace, Chloe will sing a new protest song, and I'll give an impassioned speech entitled: 'This house believes that war between werewolves and vampires is wrong.'

I'll convince both sides of their fundamental

similarities and shared values, so the wolves can return home and Vlad can withdraw his formal declaration of battle. Then everyone can shake hands and I'll get back home with two full days to revise maths.

Now all I need to do is write a speech so powerful it makes these sworn enemies look upon each other as brothers. I can only hope that the debating skills that won me the regional trophy last year haven't deserted me, because now the safety of the whole world is riding on them.

Thursday 7TH June

We were supposed to be preparing our contributions to the peace protest today, but Nigel called round to my room just after lunch to ask if I wanted to come to the arcade. He'd noticed that we'd both put computer games on our skills list and wanted to challenge me to a game of whatever they had. I was getting quite stuck with my speech, so I took him up on the offer.

It turned out to be one of those arcades with more gambling machines than games, but we managed to find one called *Sega Rally*. It was quite old, and the graphics were worse than the ones on my phone, but it was fun to race against Nigel. I thought I was good at games, but he sped off after just one lap, and got so many continues

Adventures of a Wimpy Werewolf

from one coin that the owner of the arcade came over to check the machine.

After that we tried Whack-a-Mole, where you had to hit these brown plastic things with a foam rubber hammer. I tried my hardest, but Nigel completely pwned me again, and got right to the top of the scoreboard on his first go. He won fifty tickets, although that wasn't quite enough for a pencil topper. If even a creature with supernatural speed can't win the Buzz Lightyear doll, you know it's a rip-off.

I complained that I could have whacked a lot more moles in wolf form, but I could hardly do so in an arcade with so many CCTV cameras.

Adventures of a Wimpy Werewolf

Nigel said that if we wanted a fairer comparison we should have a stone—throwing contest under the pier, where I'd be out of sight and free to transform. I thought this sounded like fun, so we made our way onto the seafront and under the rotten wooden structure.

Nigel picked up a huge rock and threw it out to sea. It flew right past the end of the pier and splashed into the sea like a depth charge. I went over to an even bigger rock and made myself transform.

As soon as I was in wolf form I forgot all about the rock. I couldn't focus on anything but the foul undead monster standing next to me. Rather than a fifteen—year—old boy, Nigel now appeared as a decrepit old man with razor—sharp teeth, saggy white skin and soulless black eyes. And rather than Lynx Africa, he smelled of mouldy graveyards and rotting flesh. All my

instincts told me to claw his head from his shoulders and rid the world of his hateful presence.

I shrank back into human form and told Nigel we should forget the contest as my back hurt. I might be liberal enough to accept vampires when I'm in human form, but as soon as I switch into primitive form, the old prejudices come right back out. It's a bit like Uncle Derek when he's had too many pints.

After that, we walked along the promenade and I chatted to Nigel about vampire life. He was only fifteen years old when he was transformed, but that was eighty-six years ago now, which means he's actually 101. No wonder my wolf self thought there was something strange about him.

I tried asking Nigel what the Second World War and the swinging sixties were like, but he said they weren't that different really. That's not hard to believe around here. It looks like the last time anything got a fresh coat of paint was 1975.

Adventures of a Wimpy Werewolf

Friday 8TH June

I'm writing this in the fishing boat on the way up to Hirta. It's quite a small boat, with a cabin at the front, where the three of us are currently perching. There's an open section behind where the fishing equipment should be, although the floor seems to be covered in flasks like the one Nigel was sipping from the other day. I'm guessing that what Nigel's dad really uses this boat for is travelling over to the mainland and harvesting human blood. It's pretty disgusting, but I don't want to dwell on that right now. I want to focus on the positives about both our species so I can finish my speech.

Adventures of a Wimpy Werewolf

We've been travelling on the open sea for ages now and we're still nowhere near Hirta. It must be miles away from mainland Scotland. No wonder Ryan is so keen to win it back for the werewolves. You could do what you like out there and no humans would ever know. And if anyone curious ever ventured out, you could lock them in the basement and add them to the menu for the next full moon party.

No, I mustn't think that way. I can triumph over my base instincts.

Nigel just asked me to fetch him a flask of type AB+ from the back, and when I couldn't find one, he said he'd have to settle for type B+ instead. I found the idea that Nigel had a favourite flavour of blood especially horrible, but I tried not to let it show. Drinking human blood is part of his culture and I mustn't judge him for it.

We can see the island now. On one side there's a sheltered bay leading up to a large plain where the battle will be fought, and on the other side is the castle where the coven lives. There's a graveyard at the back of the castle, which is weird because I thought vampires lived for ever. I hope they haven't built it especially for us.

I just asked Nigel about the graveyard and he said there aren't any bodies there, they just built it so they've got somewhere to go and brood about the tragedy of immortality. They're thinking of expanding it because it's quite hard to find any brooding space on wet or misty days.

Got here just in time! It's almost dark and we're just pulling into Hirta's bay to see the Lunar Wood Pack standing with their backs to the shore. Ryan's marching up and down in front of them, giving them some sort of battle speech. The vampires are facing them about 200 metres away, and one of them is also ranting up front. Must be Vlad.

These vampires are much more like the ones you see on TV, with huge black capes, frilly white shirts and slicked—back hair. They certainly look a lot more stylish than the wolves in their shellsuits and tracksuits. Obviously our clothing options are limited to stretchy fabrics, but I'd be lying if I said my species was winning the style war. The vampires look like they're dressed up for a private box in an opera house, whereas the wolves look like they're about to go looting in Poundstretcher.

Adventures of a Wimpy Werewolf

Behind the male vampires there's a row of female ones wearing ancient ball gowns. Even though I'm a werewolf, I have to admit they look rather attractive. Maybe if I avert the war, one of them will let me snog them and.. Woah! Wait a minute! I see what they did there. This is the seductive vampire beauty I've been warned about. I'll have to make an effort not to look at any of the vampire women from now on.

Behind the female vampires I can see three young girls who can't be more than ten or eleven. Surely even vampires aren't diabolical enough to make young girls fight in battle?

I just asked Nigel and he said one of the girls is his younger sister. He said she'd thrown a huge tantrum when her parents said she wasn't allowed to fight, and she'd ended up getting her own way as usual. He told me not to worry about it, though. She's over ninety years old and more than capable of defending herself. Vampires are so mental.

Okay, it's gone dark now: the battle can't be far off.

Adventures of a Wimpy Werewolf

I've got my speech notes, my loudhailer and my Alliance of Peaceful Supernaturals placard. It's time to get out there and increase the peace.

We marched out into the space between the armies. I waved to Ryan, who snarled with rage. Nigel waved at an older vampire, who shamefully buried his face in his hands. I'm guessing that was his dad.

Chloe turned on the loudhailer and announced that we were an alliance of vampires and werewolves and we were here to stop the battle. She said that unlike them, we wouldn't use violence to put our point across. Instead, we'd use the peaceful art forms of poetry, song and speech. This caused everyone in Ryan's pack to bark like someone had just stolen their Pedigree Chum. The vampires responded with loud hissing. It looked as though they were going to be a tough crowd.

Chloe handed Nigel the loudhailer and he read his poem:

Adventures of a Wimpy Werewolf

'Peace Please'
By Nigel Mullet, aged 101

I've got fangs
You've got fur
But that doesn't mean
There must be war

You sleep in a kennel
I don't sleep at all
But that doesn't mean
We must build a wall

I drink blood
You eat cattle
But that doesn't mean
We must go to battle

Your skin is hairy
Mine is pale white
But that doesn't mean
That we must fight

We've got our beauty
You've got your fleas
Let's live together
In harmony and peace.

Adventures of a Wimpy Werewolf

While I thought the sentiment of Nigel's poem was right, I think it's unfortunate he used so many negative stereotypes. It's simply untrue that werewolves live in kennels and have fleas, and if he'd checked his facts with me, I could have helped him deliver a more powerful piece.

The poem was greeted by silence from both sides, which I hoped was a sign of contemplation rather than embarrassment.

Next, Chloe picked up her acoustic guitar and performed her new protest song, 'Children of the Bite'.

The words were:

Adventures of a Wimpy Werewolf

'Let's join together in peace and love tonight
    Supernatural fighting just isn't right
Creatures of darkness, can't you see the light?
Underneath it all we're just children of the bite.'

Although Chloe's voice hadn't improved, I thought the song made a very good point. Both werewolves and vampires are created by bites, so shouldn't we concentrate on our similarities rather than our differences?

Unfortunately most of the werewolves howled along as Chloe began to sing, and the message got a little lost.

Chloe passed the loudspeaker to me. I took my speech notes out of my pocket, aware that it was all down to me. I was the only one who could save the world from devastation.

I clearly my throat and began my speech:

'This house believes that war between werewolves and vampires is wrong. By Luke Thorpe.

'My name is Luke and I'm a werewolf. Although I've only been one for a couple of months I've learned a lot about our culture in that time, and it's made me feel immensely proud of what I am.

'But does that mean I have to dislike that other noble supernatural creature we share this

Adventures of a Wimpy Werewolf

planet with, the vampire? Of course it doesn't. I can be proud of my species and respect yours too.

'Do I find it unpleasant that you quaff human blood like it was Ribena? Of course I do.

'Do I find it strange that you don't sleep? Of course I do.

'Does it freak me out that you're technically not even alive? Of course it does.

'But are any of these things reasons to hate you? Of course not.

'The fact is there's room for both of us on this planet. And when we meet, it doesn't have to lead to violence.

'Less than a week ago, I met Nigel here. It was the first time I'd ever met a vampire. I could

have barked at him. He could have hissed at me. But instead, we found common ground. In our case, it was a racing game from the mid-nineties called *Sega Rally* and a machine where you had to hit plastic moles with a hammer, but that's not important. The point is, we talked and we became friends.

'So as you gather on this beautiful island under this bright moon, let me ask you this: Are we really so different? Under our fur and our pale skin are we not pretty much the same? Do we really want to fight each other when we could try to get along instead? Do we really want this war?'

As my speech built to its rousing climax, I was hoping that both sides would be moved to tears of remorse and rush to greet each other in friendly embrace. Unfortunately, when I asked, 'Do we really want this war?' both sides shouted: 'Yes!' I tried responding with, 'Are we really sure about that?' and they repeated: 'Yes!'

It was at this point that the full moon made its first appearance of the night. As one, the Lunar Wood Pack hurled themselves to the floor as their pelts sprouted, their bones elongated and their muscles reformed.

When I turned to ask Chloe what we should try next,

Adventures of a Wimpy Werewolf

I saw that she was also writhing around on the floor and sprouting hairs. A minute later she was in wolf form. She stamped on her acoustic guitar, chewed the edge of her placard and rushed to join the rest of the Lunar Wood wolves. I felt like having a go at her for betraying her ideals, but I know what it's like when you transform.

The wolves let out screeching howls from their side of the battlefield, and the vampires hissed back.

I suggested to Nigel that as the only remaining members of the peace movement, we should stage a sit-in protest in the middle of the battlefield.

We sat down with our legs crossed and held up our placards. Then the two sides charged towards each other and we agreed that we might as well stage the sit-in protest on his dad's boat where we were less likely to be stampeded.

I'm writing this from the cabin inside the boat. The battle is raging outside, so I suppose I should go out and have a look. But I can't really abandon my sit-in protest here in this comfortable, safe boat. I don't think that would be the right thing to do.

Saturday 9TH June

It's now 3am and the battle is still going on. At first it sounded so fierce that I assumed everyone would be dead within minutes. But the howls, hisses and yelps didn't let up, so after a couple of hours we went out to see what was going on.

The whole battlefield was a rapid blur of violence. It was really hard to take in at first, but after a while my eyes got used to the speed and I could see the wolves attacking with tail spins, high pounces and claw slashes, while the vampires countered with powerful slaps, swift punches and sweeping kicks.

If either side had been fighting humans, the battle would have lasted about three seconds, but both sides were perfectly matched. After watching the mad frenzy for a few minutes it became apparent why vampire—werewolf battles go on for so long. Without wooden stakes and silver bullets, both creatures are virtually impossible to defeat. Werewolves have amazing strength and resilience, while vampires don't feel pain and can heal very rapidly.

In theory, a werewolf has the strength to destroy a vampire by swiping its head off, which is what Ryan had been training me to do. But they'd have to catch the vampire unawares first. And given how quickly they can block attacks, the chances of that were low.

The only wolf who was really capable of surprising the vampires was Paul the werepoodle. His tactic was to trot around the battlefield looking cute and harmless, and then pounce up to their necks. He even managed to sink his teeth into the neck of an elderly vampire while I was watching him, but he was soon wrestled off and booted to the other side of the battlefield.

Every now and then, a wolf would manage to slice off a vampire's arm, but it would just crawl back and heal

itself on again. I even saw one of these severed arms deliberately trip up the wolf who had just sliced it off, which was rather cunning.

At one point, Richard sliced both a vampire's arms off at once, but they still managed to heal themselves on again. Nigel said, 'It's just a flesh wound,' and together we recited the *Monty Python* sketch about the knight who gets all his limbs chopped off. I was pleased he was a fan too.

Perhaps the most shocking attack of all came from Nigel's little sister, Daisy. While her friends held one of the wolves down, she brushed its fur, tied pink ribbons along its back and covered its claws in red nail varnish.

It was hard to tell, but I think the wolf was Steve, the scaffolder we visited a couple of weeks ago. Poor Steve. I know he was really looking forward

to the battle. I bet he didn't expect to end up as the centrepiece of the My Little Werewolf grooming parlour.

It's now 5am and the fighting has ended for the night. No wolves or vampires have been killed, but both sides are claiming victory.

You don't get much darkness in summer this far north. The sun began to rise just before four and all the wolves transformed back. After that, Ryan led them all back to Richard's fishing trawler to rest until tonight.

We found Chloe in the middle of the battlefield. She must have transformed in the middle of battling Nigel's dad because she was making polite conversation with him. They obviously knew each other from when she was Nigel's girlfriend. She asked him if he was enjoying life on the island and he said it was nice to be away from the stress of city life, but he missed having a decent-sized graveyard to brood in. He asked about her studies and she said they were fine. Then, after an awkward silence he said he ought to be getting back to the castle.

Before he went, he asked Nigel if he could give the

poetry a rest tonight. I was going to suggest that he should encourage his son's creativity, but I didn't want to be confrontational so soon after the fighting had paused.

So now we're back on the boat, and trying to work out what to do next. I've seen nothing to make me believe that tonight's battle will be resolved one way or the other. Which means that at the end of the third battle, in just under two days' time, Ryan will bring out his wooden stakes, Vlad will bring out his silver bullets, and our races will be plunged back into full-scale war.

Nigel wants to start our next brainstorming session right away. It's all right for him; he doesn't need to sleep.

My first suggestion was that I steal the wooden stakes from Ryan's boat while Nigel steals Vlad's gun and silver bullets from the castle. Then we march into the battlefield again and threaten to kill everyone unless they sign a peace treaty.

Chloe pointed out that if they refused, we'd have to go through with it. Then we'd be the ones responsible for restarting the war, which wouldn't make us a very good peace movement.

Adventures of a Wimpy Werewolf

She suggested that we steal the weapons and threaten to use them on each other instead. Nigel could hold the pistol up to my head while I hold the stake over his heart. Then if they refused to call off the battle, we could kill each other and become glorious martyrs to our cause. Nigel and I said we were both keen to explore other options.

I've just had an idea, but I'm not sure if it breaks supernatural law. Nigel's gone to the castle library to fetch some books so we can find out.

Nigel came back with three dusty tomes about supernatural law, and we're checking through them. The one I'm reading is mainly concerned with ways in which wolves and vampires have tried to get round the silver bullet and wooden stake rules. For example, there was a coven in Canada who claimed to be hunting moose when their silver bullets ricocheted off some antlers and killed a group of werewolves. And there was a pack in Sweden who claimed to be constructing a wooden fence around their compound when a passing group of vampires slipped and fell onto the poles heart-first. Neither of these groups got away with it, but I reckon I might have more luck with my scheme.

We've gone through all the books now, and we're convinced that my plan doesn't technically break any supernatural laws. So now we're sailing to the town of Lochdale on the mainland to buy the materials we need. We're going to have to miss tonight's battle, but I'm sure it will end in stalemate again anyway. Tomorrow night's showdown is the one we need to stop.

I thought Chloe might stay behind on the island, but she doesn't want to take part in any more fighting, so we've brought her along. I've had to chain her to the back of the boat to restrain her during tonight's transformation. This is going to be awkward.

Adventures of a Wimpy Werewolf

Sunday 10TH June

I'd just drifted off to sleep for the first time in two days when the full moon rose and Chloe transformed and kicked up a massive fuss.

She immediately began to strain against her chains, rocking the little boat back and forth so violently that I thought it would capsize. Nigel told me to go out and control her, so I tried to calm her down by repeating some of the exercises from my relaxation course. This had no effect, so I tried singing her song 'Children of the Bite' in the hope that it would trigger off memories of her peace-loving human self.

This didn't work either so I had to resort to turning myself into a wolf and slapping her across the face. Now she's whimpering with fear and I'm feeling incredibly guilty, but at least the boat's safe. Yes, I know it went against the principles of our non-violent organization. It's not easy.

We now have everything we need and we're on our way back to Hirta for tonight's final showdown. We had to wait ages for the shops to open when we got to Lochdale, but I didn't mind because it gave me a chance to phone Mum.

I told her I'd seen some lovely scenery (true), made a new friend (true) and kept away from trouble (massive lie). She asked if I was still getting on well with Chloe and I said I was. She said I should enjoy love now because it only gets more complicated as you get older. What, more complicated than having to shift into the form of a wolf to stop them destroying a boat? If that's true, I don't think I'll bother with relationships at all.

Nigel's holding his cargo inside the cabin, while we're sitting out back with ours, along with all the rope and handcuffs. Nigel had to steal the latter from the local police station using his vampire speed, because the only ones they had in the shops were covered in pink fur. I feel a little guilty about this, but if they help us prevent war I'm sure it's justified.

    I apologized to Chloe for hitting her last night, but she didn't remember anything so I pretended I was joking.

Okay, we're pulling back into Hirta now. The vampires are back inside their castle while the wolves are sleeping in their trawler. It looks like the battle was particularly fierce last night, as there are lots of missing clumps of turf in the middle of the battlefield.

    It's now time to get out there and set everything up. If I never update this diary again it's because my plan failed and I'm dead. Either that or I just lost interest in writing it like I did with my blog.

As soon as we got back on land, I lugged my shopping bags over to the far side of the battlefield and spread my haul evenly across the ground. First, I took out all the garlic cloves and crushed them into the soil. Then I sprinkled the whole area with granulated garlic and

garlic seeds. I finished my preparation by emptying out all my tins of garlic and herb pasta sauce. I wasn't sure if this would contribute much, but there was a 3—for—2 offer on it, so I thought I might as well get it.

I looked across at Nigel and he gave me the thumbs—up to indicate that he'd finished spreading all the wolfsbane on the other side of the field. Then I walked a really long way back to the boat to make sure I didn't go anywhere near it.

Now we're on the boat and waiting for the armies to gather. Chloe's asked to be restrained on here again tonight, which is just as well. Even if we warned her about the trap, she'd forget when she turned wolf and run straight into it.

Just before midnight, the two armies gathered to face each other for a third and final time. Luke and

Adventures of a Wimpy Werewolf

Vlad both smirked silently in front of their armies, contemplating the destruction they were about to unleash.

A few minutes later, the clouds parted to reveal the full moon once again. The Lunar Wood Pack dropped to all fours and howled, while the vampires watched from the other side of the battlefield in disgust. Then the wolves were on their hind legs and ready to charge.

The two armies ran towards each other. But after covering just a few feet, both sides fell down to ground and screamed in agony.

My plan had worked. My garlic zone had trapped all the vampires, while Nigel's wolfsbane zone had trapped all the wolves.

I'll be the first to admit that my plan was a bit sneaky. Chloe found a rule in one of the law books forbidding the throwing of garlic and wolfsbane during battle, but it didn't say you couldn't leave them lying around.

As soon as the armies were contained within the garlic and wolfsbane zones, Nigel and I fastened their hands with the cuffs and tied their feet with the rope. I was a little worried about this part of the plan, as I thought the vampires might lash out at me when I tried to restrain them. But they were as weak as babies after their hit of garlic.

After I'd secured all the vampires, I dragged them into the middle of the battlefield, and Nigel did the same with the wolves. They all began to struggle violently as soon as they were away from the noxious substances, but the ropes and handcuffs held fast.

Then we went off to fetch our evidence.

Monday 11TH June

I've just realized I'm actually describing Monday morning by now. This is the kind of thing that happens when you stay up all night. I never liked doing it, even on New Year's Eve when Mum said I was allowed to.

When we had our evidence, we returned to address the wolves and vampires. I told them all we were very sorry for using the toxic materials and restraining them, but we'd tried music, poetry and speech and they hadn't worked. I think the wolves got the wrong idea at this point and thought we were going to perform some more music and poetry, because they started whimpering with fear.

Nigel then held up the antique pistol and silver bullets and told the werewolves that Vlad was planning to murder them all at the end of the night.

I held up the wooden stakes and told the vampires that Ryan was planning to murder them too.

The hissing and howling rose to a pitch that was too loud to shout over, so we dragged Ryan and Vlad into the middle of the crowd for their trial, and waited for the noise to die down.

I asked Vlad if he was planning to use the bullets and he said that he had every right to if werewolves were invading his island.

Nigel asked Ryan if he was planning to use the wooden stakes and he said he had every right to because Vlad had stolen the island from his ancestors.

Then the noise started up again and we had to wait ages before we could be heard.

The trial went on and on like this. I'd ask Vlad a question and he'd reply with something about how evil wolves are, then Nigel would ask Ryan a question and he'd slag off vampires in return. Then both sides would erupt into a deafening cacophony and we'd have to wait ages for them to shut up.

This continued until dawn, when all the wolves turned back into humans. Most of them didn't know what was going on, so I had to go through it all again. But they stopped howling, which in turn made the vampires hush down too.

It also meant that Chloe turned human again, so she could take over the interrogation, which I have to admit we were getting absolutely nowhere with.

She asked Ryan what evidence he had that the island actually belonged to the Lunar Wood Pack. He said he had papers in the zip pocket of his tracksuit bottoms that proved it, so I fished them out.

Chloe didn't have to examine them long before declaring them to be fake. She said they were written on sheets of modern A4 that had been yellowed with a candle to look old. Also, if they were written hundreds of years ago, why did they use modern abbreviations like '2' and 'B' and modern slang like 'vampires for the win' and 'wolves R lame so we're jacking their island LOL'?

Ryan then admitted he'd forged the documents so he could wage war on Vlad. He said that Vlad had tried to shoot him with a silver bullet when they'd lived in the same town a few years ago. He'd managed to dodge the bullet, but he'd sworn revenge. He said that he'd been a peaceful wolf until that day and would have been happy to avoid the vampires for ever if it hadn't been for this unwarranted act of aggression.

Vlad said it wasn't unwarranted because Ryan had kept doing things to wind him up like constructing crucifixes on his lawn and getting extra large portions of garlic bread delivered to his house. But then Ryan said he'd only done this because Vlad kept throwing sticks and shouting 'Fetch!' whenever he passed him on the street.

This petty squabbling went on for ages as both Ryan and Vlad tried prove the other one had instigated the feud.

Eventually, Chloe shouted over the top of them to say that she didn't care who started it. She said they'd both put their personal vendetta above the safety of

their groups and proved themselves unfit to remain in charge.

Chloe then turned to the gathered vampires and wolves and asked if these were really the kinds of leaders they wanted. Both sides grumbled for a while, but eventually admitted that they weren't.

Chloe suggested that the coven and the pack elect new leaders. She said that she could think of two young candidates with fresh energy and ideas, who'd already shown commitment to their coven and pack by saving them from death. Her speech built to a rousing climax in which she demanded that Nigel and I were sworn in as the new leaders!

I'd like to think her suggestion would have been greeted with wild applause if it weren't for the handcuffs.

After Chloe's speech, we released everyone except Ryan and Vlad, and the vampires and werewolves went off to discuss their situations separately.

I'm happy to say that there wasn't any opposition to the suggestion that I become the new pack leader. The werewolves agreed that Ryan had misled them and couldn't be trusted any more, and most of the others already have full-time jobs, so they were happy to let me do it.

The vampires also agreed to let Nigel lead their coven. While debating the matter, some of them raised the objection that he's unreliable, disorganized and obsessed with bad poetry. But then it was pointed out that the coven leader didn't have to do much except protect the island from werewolves, and that wouldn't be difficult now, so they might as well give him a chance.

As a symbol of our commitment to peace, I broke all the wooden stakes in half and Nigel smashed up Vlad's pistol with a rock. He was going to smash up the silver bullets too, but I was worried that he might accidentally send one of them flying into a wolf and the war would have to start after all.

Nigel's sister then created a peace treaty using her calligraphy set. I thought she did a good job, although it could have done without the Justin Bieber stickers and glitter.

As we were signing it, Nigel said he'd been confident all along that our plan would work. It wasn't our plan, it was my plan! I don't want to be petty at a time like this, but a little credit wouldn't have gone amiss. The best idea Nigel came up with in our brainstorming session was to give free pencil cases to the wolves and vampires if they agreed to stop the battle.

Adventures of a Wimpy Werewolf

After that, we drew up formal notices of exclusion for Ryan and Vlad to sign. Under the terms of our agreement, they're free to join other packs and covens, but they must never return to ours.

We then released them and ordered them to leave the island together in a small rowing boat. I was really scared that Ryan would claw my head off my shoulders to get revenge, but there wasn't much he could do with the whole pack against him.

He said that he regretted ever helping us and that he should have just left us to cope alone and see how we liked it when we woke up with our parents' intestines in our mouths. Then he started muttering about how everything would have been fine if he hadn't opened the pack up to bloody students. I was going to defend myself, but I decided to let him have his little moment. Unlike in school, there are times in real life when it's better not to reply to insults.

Adventures of a Wimpy Werewolf

After that, Ryan squeezed into the tiny boat next to Vlad and rowed away. I felt guilty about stealing his job and his home, but I had to remind myself that he'd betrayed the trust of the pack and deserved his punishment.

Nigel then announced that we were throwing the first-ever joint vampire and werewolf party starting at the castle right away. Unfortunately, neither group was very keen. Most of the werewolves said they were in a hurry to get home, and several of the vampires pretended they had to go to bed, which was an especially lame excuse for creatures that don't need to sleep.

Never mind. We might not be able to make wolves and vampires like each other, but at least we made them tolerate each other. And after centuries of clawing and hissing, that's not bad going.

We are now travelling back to Northport on Richard's trawler. I've said goodbye to Nigel, which is a shame as we were getting on quite well. I still find it bizarre that I managed to make friends with a bloodsucking vampire who was born before the *Titanic* sank. It just goes to show that we're all just people deep down inside.

Adventures of a Wimpy Werewolf

Actually that's not true at all. Neither of us are
people. I keep forgetting.

I'm sitting in the cabin next to Richard as I write
this. Everyone else is stretched out asleep on deck. I
wish I could join them, but that's not an option. I've
got my maths exam at 1.45pm tomorrow and I haven't
touched my revision notes yet.

Tuesday 12TH June

Richard has just handed me the keys to Lunar Hall,
which Ryan left in the boat. I'll pop over and start
sorting through everything as soon as I've finished my
exam and caught up on my sleep.

I still can't get over being pack leader. If I wanted I
could just order someone to fetch me another can of Red
Bull from the fridge and they'd have to do it.

No, I won't abuse my power. That's how corrupt leaders like Vlad and Ryan start. Anyway, on with the revision!

Steve just asked me if I knew why he had a scrap of pink cloth tied to his hair. I said he must have torn it from the lining of a vampire's cape in battle, and he seemed happy. I didn't have the heart to tell him it was because he was beaten up by ten-year-old girls.

We're just pulling into Northport now. The pack set off from here last Friday, so their cars are still in the long-stay parking. Alex has very kindly offered to give me a lift straight to the exam hall in his police car.

I'm inside the police car now. Alex has had to put his siren on to get me there on time, which is very exciting, although it's making my revision harder.

Adventures of a Wimpy Werewolf

We pulled up outside the exam hall with just three minutes to spare. Mr Landis saw me getting out of the police car and said he'd warned me this would happen if I tried to be cool.

I ran into the hall, opened my paper and scanned through the questions. It was fine. I could do them. I looked up at the clock. I had an hour. Everything was going to be all right. I just needed to rest my eyes for a second, and then I'd whizz through it.

I opened my eyes and looked up at the clock again. I now had ten minutes left. How had no one noticed that I'd been asleep for almost all the exam? I looked over at the invigilators, who were messing with their phones.

I picked up my pen and tried to race through the answers in the remaining minutes. I managed to get about halfway through before the paper was snatched away. I reckon the best mark I can get now is a 'C'.

After my exam, I came home, told Mum I'd had a lovely youth hostelling trip and ran right upstairs to bed.

Wednesday 13TH June

I've just woken up after eighteen hours' sleep. That's the longest since I had my appendix out.

The more I think about my exams, the more I think I'm going to get Cs and Ds rather than As and A stars, even when you take my excellent coursework into account. But I don't really mind. The knowledge that I helped save the world from apocalypse is reward enough for me. I wonder if you can get a Duke of Edinburgh award for that.

It doesn't matter anyway. I'm already in a leadership role, which means more to me than any amount of A stars could have done. I've been placed in a position of responsibility and I don't want to disappoint those who are counting on me.

For most of my classmates, the hard work is now over and they've got a couple of months off to watch TV, play their games consoles and generally faff about. For me, the real work starts, as I'm going to forge a new era for the Lunar Wood Pack.

Adventures of a Wimpy Werewolf

Thursday 14ᵀᴴ June

I went round to Lunar Hall this morning and had a root around. The good news is that Ryan stashed all the pack's money under the floorboards, as he didn't trust banks. And now the defence budget has been slashed to zero, I'm sure we can do something constructive with all those grubby piles of notes.

In the afternoon Chloe came round and we had a brainstorming session about how to use the funds. We both agreed that the house should be more than just a place wolfpeople come for monthly transformations. It should be somewhere they can drop by whenever they want to discuss wolf issues.

So we've officially changed the name of Lunar Hall to Lunar Wood Lupine Community Centre. One of the first rules we're going to establish is that the pack must now refer to lycanthrophy as their 'gift' rather than their 'condition' or their 'disease'. If we're to behave more positively as wolves, we need to start by thinking more positively about ourselves.

Friday 15TH June

Chloe brought the Ikea catalogue round this afternoon and we chose some new furniture for Lunar Wood Lupine Community Centre. We've decided to plaster over all the holes in the walls, give all the rooms a repaint and buy everyone a personalized bowl for their raw meat.

We've also decided to make a wall collage about werewolf diversity, with pictures of bears, poodles and lions as well as wolves. The message of this is that there's no right or wrong way to transform, and all wolf forms are equally valid.

In addition, Chloe wants to replace all the light bulbs with energy-saving ones so we can do our bit for the planet. You'd think that by saving the planet from apocalypse we've already done quite a bit, but you can never really do enough. Especially if you're planning to live until the middle of the next century.

    This afternoon, we wrote up the ideas from yesterday's brainstorm and sent them out to the pack:

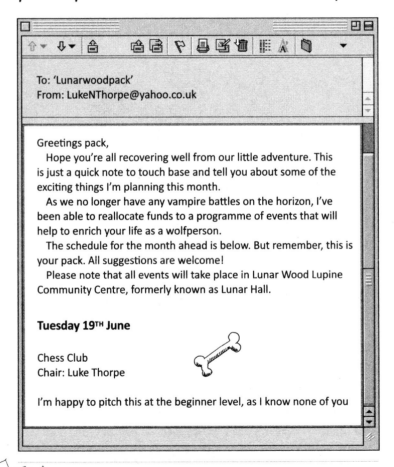

To: 'Lunarwoodpack'
From: LukeNThorpe@yahoo.co.uk

Greetings pack,

    Hope you're all recovering well from our little adventure. This is just a quick note to touch base and tell you about some of the exciting things I'm planning this month.

    As we no longer have any vampire battles on the horizon, I've been able to reallocate funds to a programme of events that will help to enrich your life as a wolfperson.

    The schedule for the month ahead is below. But remember, this is your pack. All suggestions are welcome!

    Please note that all events will take place in Lunar Wood Lupine Community Centre, formerly known as Lunar Hall.

Tuesday 19TH June

Chess Club
Chair: Luke Thorpe

I'm happy to pitch this at the beginner level, as I know none of you

are fanatics. But come along and I guarantee you'll get hooked. And if you aren't, we can always play Connect Four instead.

Thursday 21ST June

Book Group
Chair: Chloe Sparrow

Chloe will be leading a discussion on *The Strange Case of Dr Jekyll and Mr Hyde* by Robert Louis Stevenson. Is it a realistic portrayal of people who turn into violent monsters?

Adventures of a Wimpy Werewolf

Tuesday 26ᵀᴴ June

Debating Society
Chair: Luke Thorpe

Chloe will argue for the motion: 'This house believes werewolves should reveal themselves to humanity and ask for their understanding,' while Luke will argue against it.

Thursday 28ᵀᴴ June

Werewolf Encounter Group
Chair: Chloe Sparrow

A chance to talk to others in confidence about the issues arising from wolf life. This week's group will focus on guilt, anger and hatred of cats.

Saturday 30ᵀᴴ June

Ultra-rare BBQ
Chairs: Luke Thorpe and Chloe Sparrow

Come round for a barbecue with a difference – we won't be turning it on! Be prepared to enjoy plenty of lamb, beef and pork as nature intended – raw. Yum yum!

Monday 2ND July

Wolfwoman Support Group
Chair: Chloe Sparrow

A discussion group dedicated to
the empowerment of female pack
members. This first session will
deal with the topics of whether
wolf society is inherently
sexist and which are the
most effective hair-removal
treatments.

Wednesday 4TH July

Werewolf Religious Study Group
Chair: Luke Thorpe

This group will explore issues relating to religion and lycanthrophy.
In this first session we'll discuss whether it's possible to be both
a werewolf and a Christian. And if so, should we be exempt from
the commandments about not killing people and coveting our
neighbour's ox?

Adventures of a Wimpy Werewolf

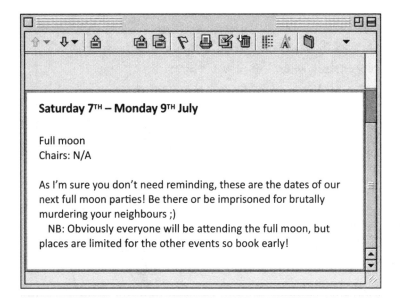

Saturday 7ᵀᴴ – Monday 9ᵀᴴ July

Full moon
Chairs: N/A

As I'm sure you don't need reminding, these are the dates of our next full moon parties! Be there or be imprisoned for brutally murdering your neighbours ;)
   NB: Obviously everyone will be attending the full moon, but places are limited for the other events so book early!

Saturday 16ᵀᴴ June

I've already received nineteen responses to my email. Admittedly, they were all bookings for the ultra-rare BBQ. And the only suggestion for further activities was that we should get sky so we can show Premiership matches, but it's a start. I could always fold the chess club and the debating society into the football evening if that's what people want. That's the kind of flexible leader I am.

I went round to Lunar Wood Lupine Community Centre this afternoon and tried to teach myself to be more responsible when I'm in wolf form.

For all his faults, Ryan did a very good job at restraining the pack from killing humans. I remember the night he howled at us when we tried to eat the stranded motorists. That will be my responsibility next time it happens. If I can't hold them back, there's going to be a lot of dismembered humans around, and the finger of suspicion will eventually be pointed at those with thick eyebrows and a taste in undercooked meat.

I went out into the garden and laid out a sheep carcass with a coat on to represent a stranded motorist and a picture of Mahatma Gandhi to represent the values of tolerance and restraint. Then I transformed and tried to make myself choose the photo over the sheep.

I can't pretend it was a great success. I instinctively went for the sheep the first five times I changed. I didn't even touch the Gandhi photo until the sixth time, and that was only because I got confused and thought he was really there and I could bite his throat. But I've got to try. I was a prefect for over fourteen months. It must have taught me something about discouraging anti-social behaviour.

Sunday 17TH June

I was cleaning out one of the downstairs rooms today when I came across a stack of Ryan's papers. It looks like he kept some sort of diary too, although the writing isn't very clear, and most of what I can make out details his obsessive hatred for Vlad. But I did find one very interesting entry:

'Looks like the ginger kid is coming through 4 me. Saw him in L wood today, changing 2 weeks before full moon. Finally got an alpha. Knew he would be, was sure the day I bit him. Gave him my email, pretended 2 B casual but followed his scent so I know where 2 call if he doesn't show. Good timing for attack on V.'

I've read through this a few times now, and I'm pretty sure Ryan means he's the one who turned me into a wolf in the first place. And the odd thing is, he deliberately targeted me because his instinct told him I'd become an alpha wolf.

When I think back to what I was like a few months

ago, I wonder what he could possibly have seen in me. I can't believe anyone could have guessed I'd become the most powerful type of shape—shifter.

I suppose I owe Ryan my thanks for seeing my potential and for biting me. It's been difficult and frightening at times, but I wouldn't go back to being a boring human for the world.

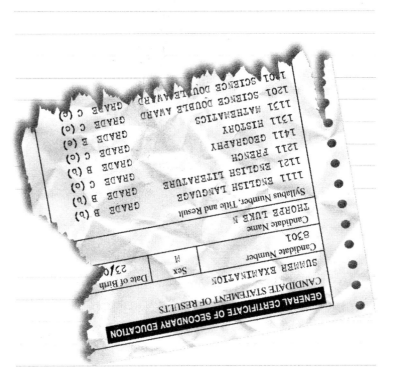

GENERAL CERTIFICATE OF SECONDARY EDUCATION

CANDIDATE STATEMENT OF RESULTS

SUMMER EXAMINATION

	Sex	Date of Birth
	M	23/0

Candidate Number
8301

Candidate Name
THORPE LUKE N

Syllabus Number, Title and Result	
1111 ENGLISH LANGUAGE	GRADE B (b)
1121 ENGLISH LITERATURE	GRADE B (b)
	GRADE C (c)
1211 FRENCH	GRADE B (b)
1411 GEOGRAPHY	GRADE C (c)
1311 HISTORY	GRADE B (e)
1731 MATHEMATICS	GRADE C (c)
1201 SCIENCE DOUBLE AWARD	GRADE C (c)
1201 SCIENCE DOUBLE AWARD	

Adventures of a Wimpy Werewolf